The Redwood Forest

Sarah Gage Weber

This book is dedicated to every person who was, or still is, living in Humboldt County. We are a rare and special breed, my friends.

Disclaimer

Some of the scenes in this book are sensitive in nature, thus reader discretion is advised.

Chapter 1

When crazy runs generations back in your family, you can't help but feel that some day, some how, you're going to fall down that rabbit hole along with every other poor family member.

I feel like I'm driving down that rabbit hole right now as I maneuver my car through redwood trees as tall as buildings...Even taller, if I'm being perfectly honest. I'm driving back to my hometown in Humboldt County, California, where the closest we had to any kind of "skyscraper" was the county jail. And that was maybe three floors tall. Humboldt was not about the majesty of concrete jungles.

No, the majesty here in Humboldt came from the trees, so dense and large you felt like a woodland nymph or a Naiad when walking amongst them. I played that game a lot when I was a kid. But the trees that once held so much mystique and enchantment to me now seem to be reaching their branches out to grab hold of me and pull me into their gangling canopy.

I haven't been back to Eureka, the county seat of Humboldt, in eight years. Being the daughter of a neurotic mother and a drunk father was reason enough to stay away. The second I graduated from high school, I dropped Eureka like a bad habit and tried to shlep off years of backwoods mannerisms by way of the provocative charisma of New York City.

The murky sunlight filters down through the trees, giving the road, my car and even me an eerily viridescent tinge, like I've been dunked into a mossy pond. I try to block the thoughts from my head with some oldies tunes, but all it's really doing is reminding me of what I'm driving back to. As it happens, Creedence Clearwater Revival croons on about going around the bend…

"'Hitch a ride to the end of the highway where the neons turn to wood'… Jesus Christ," I say to myself, feeling the first of many shivers run the length of my body. I try to shake them off with, "It wasn't all bad." A small pacifier.

It's true, though. It hadn't always been bad. But when the economy crashed in 2007, the town of Eureka went to hell in a hand-basket.

And my family shortly followed suit. My mother was always a little off her rocker, but once the economy crashed, her oddball behavior increased ten-fold. She suffered bipolar rants, hallucinations, rages…This all intermixed with what was once a loving—albeit strange—mother. In my later years, interacting with her was next to impossible because you never knew if "Good Mama" or "Bad Mama" would come out.

This was also about the time my dad started drinking much more heavily than he used to. I think he did it because he couldn't handle watching my mother dive into the deep end of the pool, but that's just a theory. I'd never really had a chance to ask him. He passed away a few years ago. I have to wonder if he would have told me. While he was a generous and kind man, he spoke very little. Unless it was about history, that is, World War I to be exact. And no doubt living on ten acres that had to be managed like a farm was enough to keep him up to his nose in distractions.

And since mental illness was imminent in *his* mother, I have no doubt he was living out the hell of his childhood all over again. This was as good enough a reason to drink until blind drunk as any, in my opinion. He never spoke of his mom much, only to cryptically say that she "wasn't right." I was smart enough to catch on and not string up a litany of questions.

4

The whole reason I'm driving back to this God-forsaken place is because my mother has finally passed away and I get the lovely job of clearing out the house and figuring out what the hell to do with the accumulation of detritus she's left behind. I know I sound like an ungrateful brat, but the fact of the matter is, this is a blessing. She was unfit to live by herself so she had a caretaker living with her full-time whom she regularly harassed. I'd get calls from Daisy in the middle of the night, crying and complaining about some other tirade my mother had unleashed upon her. I had to increase Daisy's pay three times over the past two years just to keep her on board.

I can feel my eyes getting tired, no doubt from driving this U-Haul for days on end. I have no idea what can be salvaged from our old house, but I do know that at least a few items I will want to keep, like the seven foot grandfather clock my mother's father had salvaged from a pile (literally) of crap on some farm years and years ago. I can only imagine what some of the other stories my parents' furniture could tell.

I see a gas station sign and decide to pull over for some cheap coffee and a little walk. Driving across the country was a hell of a lot easier back when I was eighteen. I didn't know that at twenty-six years old my bones could creak and crack like an old woman's might. I've got maybe an hour left before I reach my destination, and I'm quite certain I could make it there sans coffee. But I think I'm just biding my time—procrastinating—staving off the inevitable.

I turn off the highway and slow the van to a crawl. (More procrastinating.) I pull into a slot and kill the engine, gathering in my surroundings before I exit the car.

"You're not in Kansas anymore, Emma," I say to myself as I watch a dowdy, overweight woman reprimand her small boy by tugging on his arm and spitting harsh words into his face. I think I make out a "brat" and a "stupid boy," but I can't be sure. I guess my ears don't want to hear that kind of talk, especially directed at something that can't defend itself.

I'm no virgin when it comes to harsh language, since New York, however magnificent, can be pretty brutal. But it still saddens me to see a "Bush Country Mom" humiliate her kid.

I exit the cab and stretch out my legs, feeling like I've already grown an inch simply by standing. I eye Bush Mom as I make towards the convenience store adjacent to the gas pumps. She gives me a snarky glare, making a point to look me up and down like *I'm* something *she* would step in.

Just because your purse's Coach don't mean you're better than me, is what I imagine she's thinking.

I slip into the store, a tinkling of bells notifying the employee that someone's arrived. I see the attendant, who can't be more than eighteen, stop what he's doing to stare at me.

Am I really that out of place?

I glance down at my outfit as I utilize the coffee machine. It's not like I've got "couture" written across my butt or anything, just simple cropped jeans and a white blouse. I'm even wearing sandals! If I remember correctly, those and Ugg boots are like the native footwear around here…besides hiking shoes, of course.

I shake off my insecurities and grab a bottled water along with my coffee, head over to the counter, and drop everything in front of the boy who hasn't stopped staring at me this whole time.

"Is this all for you?" He asks, his voice breaking in an adorably prepubescent way.

"Yes, thank you."

"Are you moving out or moving in?" he asks, nodding his chin towards the U-Haul. I catch a hint of a Hispanic accent.

"Oh…uh…Just passing through, actually."

"Oh." He rings me up and takes my cash without another word. A conversationalist he is not.

I make my way back towards the car feeling like I have a bullseye on my back. It's not a crowded gas station, but it still feels as though many sets of eyes rest on me.

There are no words to describe how uncomfortable I feel; a feeling, I realize, I'm going to have to get comfortable with.

~~~

My family's property is located just outside of town, out in an area known as Freshwater. As I turn onto Pigeon Point Road, my mind shifts back to when I was a kid, when running around the property through the redwoods was an all-out adventure. I'd pretend to be a lost fairy trying to find her way home. I remember my mother had made me a special pair of wings out of paper, lace and glitter, telling me that with these "enchanted wings," I would always find my way home.

"It would appear so, Mom," I say to no one.

The beginning of Pigeon Point Road is pretty well populated, but the farther back I drive, the houses—houses I remember from so long ago—get fewer and farther between until it's just trees. Huge trees. It's somewhat jarring.

In fact, so jarred am I that I nearly miss our house's driveway. The road isn't paved and the narrowness unnerves me with this huge hunk of a car I'm driving. The trees look like they've grown even more, encroaching on the road like they don't want visitors to enter. And maybe they don't. Clearly no work has been done on keeping this drive clear. Large branches crunch under my tires and scrape against the side of the van. It sounds like nails on a chalkboard, making the hair on the back of my neck instinctively stand up.

It's like a punch to the gut when I see my house. It sits in a clearing of trees like a huge whitehead might sit on someone's forehead. It's a boxy house, with a first and second story deck decorating the front. The white clapboards are peeling and dingy looking. The pitched roof is littered with redwood leaves that overflow into the rain gutters, giving me a headache just thinking about trying to clean that out. The yard is ridiculously overgrown, adding more pressure to my headache.

If I'm being honest here, I'd say the damn house looks haunted. Even though my mother passed away just last week, it looks like this house hasn't been inhabited in decades and that just depresses me. Not that it was Daisy's job to do maintenance, but it would have been nice to know in advance that it had been falling into such disrepair.

I park the U-Haul and step out, my nose instantly assaulted with the smell of redwoods trees. It's not an unpleasant smell, per se, but it's a smell I've been running from for eight years.

I turn in a slow circle, surveying the property.

I heave a sigh.

"This is gonna suck."

Dread forms in my stomach as I envision all those ghosts I've been running from. I see them rushing out the front door to clobber me. Before I can stop it, my body lets off a knee-jerk shudder.

"Oh, for crying out loud, it's just a house! Your childhood house, no less. You should be thankful you even had a roof over your head in the first place." I figure admonishing myself will keep the dread down as I grab my suitcase from the passenger seat and pull out my house key. Honestly, I was surprised I even found it.

I had worried that I'd thrown it away in one of my many "purges," but I guess something inside me had known to keep it.

I wade through the overgrown grass and walk up the three steps to the porch, feeling like I'm ten years old again coming home from a sleepover at Heidi's, my best friend all through school. Thinking of her sends a sharp pain through my heart. She'd been crushed when I told her I was moving to New York, so crushed in fact that I haven't spoken to her in years. Same as Bryan...

"Maybe that's something I can fix as well," I whisper as I slide the key in the door and unlock it. I gulp a huge breath, like somehow that will fortify my nerves. All it does is make me want to belch.

"Time to face the music." I'm embarrassed to hear my voice shake.

Chapter 2

The air is so stale and still that when I enter the front door, it feels like I'm walking into a brick wall. The curtains in every room have been shut tight, making the whole house feel secluded and unused.

The entryway and staircase are the first thing you see when you walk through the door. To the left is the living room, with its huge stone fireplace that looks like a gaping mouth. To the right is the dining room that connects to the large farm-style kitchen.

The grandfather clock ticks monotonously from the living room, reminding me that, no, time does not stand still around here…even though it feels like it should.

I place my suitcase at the base of the stairs and slowly walk the first floor, opening curtains and windows, trying my hardest to tamp down the memories that want to come rushing up. Every room has a story, multiple stories, and until I'm well and sufficiently drunk, I don't want to remember those stories.

As I enter the kitchen I notice a single sheet of paper resting on the spotless countertop.

Dear Emma,

Here is my house key. I tried to tidy up as best I could. If you need anything, I'm living in town. Take care of yourself out here!

Sincerely, Daisy

She left me her phone number, for which I'm grateful. At least I have *someone* to talk to around here. On a whim, I send her a quick text letting her know I'm in town and at the house.

    With nothing left for me downstairs, I grab my suitcase and head upstairs. The second floor houses all of the bedrooms, three to be exact, and two bathrooms. I walk down the hall towards my old bedroom, amazed that the stickers I put on the door when I was a kid are still there, albeit faded. My Little Pony and Strawberry Shortcake welcome me.

I'm even more amazed that not a single thing has changed in my room. The bed is still made up with my floral-pattered comforter, Eddy the Teddy Bear sitting sentinel on the pillows. My desk still has its pictures and random boxes of jewelry. My bookshelf still holds all my textbooks, trophies, picture frames…It's like my parents left this room as my shrine after I deserted Humboldt County. A scruple of guilt forms in my heart.

"What about all your stuff, Emma? You need to at least bring some of it!" My mom had cried.

"I don't need it. I don't want it."

I remember the big, fat tears that had streaked down her face as she hugged me fiercely, Dad on the sidelines watching with a creased brow, his only indication as to how much it hurt to see me leave.

Had I always been such a little shit?

I squash that thought down and dump my suitcase on the bed. I don't feel like unpacking. I do feel like opening up this house as much as possible, lighting all the dark corners so the ghosts won't get me. The only room I avoid is my parents' bedroom. I'm not sure why, but I keep the door closed, certain that when I open it, the ghouls will attack.

~~~

Daisy had cleaned out the refrigerator, so there is absolutely nothing for me to eat. *Awesome.* And then I realize that my only vehicle is the boxy U-Haul. *Double awesome.*

But I need food…and alcohol. After Dad passed away and Daisy came on board, she told me Mom had thrown out every single bottle of booze she could find, raving that it was "the Devil's elixir" and that if she didn't get rid of it all, the devil himself would come back and get her. What had shocked me most was the "come back" part…When did the devil himself *first* visit?

I decide to head to the store in town and grab some essentials. I glance at my watch and see that I have a good hour before the sun starts to set. I really don't want to drive the U-Haul down our road in the dark.

I lock up the house, nominally pleased to see that with the curtains and windows open, it doesn't seem as foreboding from the outside.

The drive into town feels like it takes forever. I relinquish the classic music for something a little more upbeat, finding the radio station I used to listen to in high school. In those days, if I wasn't listening to my dad's oldies station, I was basking in the glory of Britney Spears and The Backstreet Boys. As it is, TLC serenades me on what makes a man a "scrub." It's kind of ironic that even the radio stations around here have that frozen-in-time feeling. Shouldn't this station be playing music that is popular today? Not from a decade ago?

Eureka hasn't changed much, and that's putting it delicately. There are some new structures, but for the most part it's the same, if perhaps a little more run down in some places. It depresses me to see my hometown still in a slump. But I guess when logging, fishing and weed is all you produce, times can be hard.

I pull into the Safeway parking lot, my mind flashing to when Dad and I would grocery shop together and all the clerks knew him by name because he was that methodical and personable. It was like, "NORM!" from *Cheers* every time he walked through the doors.

I get nothing of a greeting as I walk into its chilled interior. I grab a cart and keep my eyes to the floor as I start my search. It doesn't take long before memory takes over and I know instinctively where to go for milk, produce, meat, wine...

Before long my cart is full and I'm standing in line staring at the magazine rack because I don't want to meet eyes with anyone lest they recognize me. Who knew I was such a coward? I occupy myself with pointless celebrity gossip until a voice breaks my concentration.

"How are you doing today, dear?" the old checker asks me as he starts ringing up my many, many purchases. He gives me a warm smile.

"I'm good, thank you." Since I've barely used my voice all day, it comes out sounding scratchy.

"Beautiful day, isn't it? It's a rare one around here."

I smile and nod because I know all too well what the weather is like in the summer months in Humboldt County—Eureka, specifically. It sucks, plain and simple. While places like Kneeland and even farther south like Garberville actually get sunshine and heat, Eureka gets fog, clouds, and cold. It always seemed so unfair, especially in my younger years before I could drive myself out of it. This reminds me of when Heidi and I would climb into her little droptop Miata and drive to Willow Creek for some real summer sunshine. The thought brings a small smile to my face. I bask in this memory as the checker, whose name is Chuck, finishes ringing everything up.

"You're total is $150.56," Chuck says.

I hand him my debit card and chance looking around me. No one is paying me any notice…Except the bagger whom I catch staring at my butt. *Nice.*

"Bell? As in Ronald and Evelyn Bell's daughter?"

Son-of-a-bitch! I curse small towns.

I give him a tight smile as I say, "One in the same. How did you know my parents?"

"Ah," he laughs, the corners of his hazel eyes crinkling good-naturedly. "That's the beauty of small-town living, isn't it?" He gives me a wink. "Actually, Ron taught my son history at the high school and Evelyn…" He squints, trying to remember. "She was a nurse at the hospital, yes?" He smiles proudly at remembering these bijou details.

"That sounds about right." *At least until Dad started drinking and Mom went crazy.*

"I'm very sorry to hear about them…They were good people." He hands my card back and helps Butt Boy load my bags into the cart. "Good to see you, Emma. Hope to see you again."

I smile and nod, feeling the beginnings of a sweat break out over my brow.

I don't relish the idea of a public panic attack, so I practically run for my car and then all but screech out of the parking lot. I'm not even entirely sure why I'm on the verge of a panic attack. It was inevitable that I would come across someone who knew them…knew them before the slow decline into insanity. Maybe that's why my heart wants to jump out of my chest. It hurts to be reminded of what they once were, happy and successful. Until the recession at the beginning of my junior year…

The Cranberries sing from the radio, warning me not to linger. Sound advice for any number of the memories that tackle my brain.

After the recession, Dad stayed on at the high school, but Mom…It started as a sabbatical. The hospital had thought that a little time off would be enough to get her back in working order. Such was not the case. She slipped further and further down the rabbit hole and yet refused to give up a few shifts a week. I still don't know how she managed that. Dad receded into the background with a bottle permanently glued to his hand every day after school.

I spent more and more time at Heidi's…

And then Bryan's…

I shove that thought down and focus on the road.

~~~

The first thing I do when I get home is pop the cork to the first of many bottles of wine purchased. The sun is just starting to set and I feel an inkling of panic at spending my first night in this house after so many years away. I remind myself that the wine will help temper that.

I pour a glass and proceed to put away my groceries. I bought enough food for at least a week, since I have no idea how long I'll actually be here. I'm lucky in that my work was flexible in giving me time off. I write for a large pet product company based in New York. I busted my hump to get all my articles written before I left so I wouldn't have to worry about deadlines while in Eureka. That, at least, earned me some points from my boss.

I grab my glass and go to sit on the front porch. I know I should start boxing and organizing my parents' house, but with the dying light and lack of motivation, I decide getting drunk is a better use of my time.

I close my eyes and imagine myself as a little girl, fairy wings strapped to my back as Heidi and I run through the woods. I can almost hear our laughter. We would spend hours out in these woods, building forts and makeshift tree-houses, always finding a reason to "just stay out a little bit longer." We would rarely spend time in the house but when we did, we would play with Mom and Dad, who were always ready with some kind of game. We'd sit in the living room and just laugh. The image is so…familial. So normal.

Heidi was more like a sister to me than anything else, and since Mom had to have a hysterectomy a year after I was born, I was never graced with a sibling. So when I met Heidi in the first grade, my parents took to her almost as keenly as I did.

I take a sip of wine and look down at my phone, wondering if I should call Heidi. Would she even want to talk to me? Do I even have her current number?

A swift breeze blows my hair in my face. Now that the sun is setting, the air is getting colder, so I head back inside. I stand in the entryway and wonder what I should do with myself. It's so quiet…too quiet.

I head into the living room and switch on the TV. Having noise makes me feel better…I also go about turning on lights. Light and sound…I realize that is the only way I'm going to survive the task of cleaning out my parents' house. I've become so used to the constant drone of New York City that the quiet of Eureka feels like it could be my undoing.

I flip to the evening news and turn up the volume so I can hear it from the kitchen. I'm going to make myself some dinner, continue drinking, and maybe, just maybe, I can pass out and not give myself a panic attack.

~~~

I'm three quarters through my bottle of wine. I've finished dinner, cleaned up, and am now sitting on the couch watching Animal Planet. The wind has picked up, rattling the windowpanes and my nerves right along with them.

Even Dr. Jeff isn't a good enough distraction, so I decide to text Mia, a friend I met in college.

It's only after I've fired off a desperate-sounding plea that I realize with the time difference she will likely be asleep. *Damn.*

I dump the rest of the wine into my glass and pray this will be the glass to put me under.

My phone dings at me.

- Hey Girl! How you holding up?!

I breathe a sigh of relief.

- You're awake!? I thought you'd be in bed by now!

- Nope...I'm caught in a work deadline :(So how are you?

- I've been better...weird to be back.

- I'm sure!

- Feels like there's ghosts all around me.

- That's because there probably are! You have GOT to put that place to rest, dude. Make your amends and come home!

She has a good point. But that doesn't stop me from texting her the middle finger emoji...followed by a kissyface.

- Get some rest, sweetie. Text me tomorrow! xoxox

I shut off my phone, feeling only marginally better. I get up and walk towards the window that faces the front yard. I watch as the treetops dance around in the wind. The clouds have covered the moon, so it's black as death out there, making me shiver. I've very aware of being very alone in an old house that has no security system.

"Stop freaking yourself out, Emma!" I say to my reflection in the window. *But if someone were out there, I'd never be able to see them...*

"Oh my God! Knock it off!" I turn away from the window in a huff. "I'm going to bed. The sooner I sleep the sooner this's over with."

I gulp some wine and start turning off the TV and the lights, until all of downstairs is shrouded in darkness. I turn on the light over the stairs and head towards my bedroom, wine glass in hand.

I kinda see why Dad did this...It's almost enough to just hold the glass...almost. A big drinker I am not. At least, not up until today...

I finish off my wine while I get ready for bed. I have half a mind to open another bottle, but when I trip and slam my head into the wall, I decide one bottle is enough.

I turn off the light and take a moment to waver in front of the window. I feel like I'm swaying just like the tops of those trees. My room always had a pretty view of the redwood forest and since it's dark in my room, I'm better able to see into the night. The trees dance almost seductively, making my mind flash to that first time I danced with Bryan...

I snap my eyes away from the trees and fall into my bed, snuggling Eddy to my chest.

Take on one obstacle at a time, Emma.

Chapter 3

When I come to in the morning, I'm greeted with a very grey sky and cotton mouth. I'd been worried I'd have nightmares my first night here, but I guess the wine did its job because I slept in black oblivion the entire night. I'm sure the dead silence of the forest helped also.

I roll out of bed and go to stand at the window. Low fog sits on the ground like a thick blanket, obscuring the trunks of the redwoods. It's so bleak-looking that I wish I could crawl back into bed and sleep with Eddy all day, but I know I can't do that. The sooner I get this house packed up, the sooner I can leave.

And what better room to start on than my own.

But first…coffee.

~~~

After coffee and a shower I feel halfway human again.

I go to the U-Haul and start dragging out box after box. I also brought a ton of packing tape and bubble wrap. You can never be too prepared.

There's some stuff I want to keep, but for the most part I'm ready to just trash my room. I spend the whole morning pulling clothes from the closet and dresser, pointlessly wondering why I wasn't constantly getting sick in high school. Heidi and I would always run around wearing short shorts and tank tops, even when the weather was like it is today…*How did my parents let me get away with that?*

I can't help but blush as my brain reminds me of the looks I'd get from Bryan, flirting with our eyes from across the high school courtyard…

Once I'm done with my clothes, I move on to my bookcase. I have absolutely no reason to keep trophies from my glory jock days, but it still saddens me to see

19

them end up in the trash. And what's interesting is that despite how long I've been running from my past, I simply can't get rid of my yearbooks or photo albums. I can't bring myself to look in any of them right now, but maybe after a few glasses of wine.

The framed photos I remove from their tacky, cheap frames. There's one of me as a baby, my parents smiling into the camera as they both hold me up like some kinda of delicate prize. There's one of me and Heidi, my paper wings in place, as Mom captured us at the exact perfect moment we came running out of the redwoods holding hands and laughing. The utter joy on my face actually makes my eyes tear up...*Since when did I become so square?*

Since junior year, my mind whispers at me.

The picture I've been avoiding looking at since I got here is now in my hands.

It's a picture of Bryan. One of our favorite pastimes as a couple was to drive up to Kneeland and take pictures. I remember Bryan being a bit of a photog, but if I'm being honest here, I wasn't so bad either.

Hence, this picture. His handsome, smiling face is tilted down and to the side, like I'd just said something to make him blush. The shadows that fall across his face highlight his high cheekbones and strong jaw. He's not looking at the camera, but I can see his beautiful blue eyes twinkling all the same.

I bite back a sob as I place the photo face down in my junior yearbook...The year I took it. The year my whole world shifted...

I jump up from my seat on the floor, wiping at my eyes.

"Get a hold of yourself, Emma."

With renewed resolve, I start a fervent tackle on my desk, pulling papers from the drawers and dumping them into a trash bag if they hold no interest. I pause as I pull out a manila folder. I flip it open and nearly drop the contents on the floor. Poems. Love poems from Bryan. The one on top screams up at me. "Anywhere With You," it's titled. I read the first few lines before I snap my eyes · away. I toss the folder but keep the poems, tucking "Anywhere With You" into my yearbook along with Bryan's picture.

"Don't do that to yourself, Emma," I chide myself. Maybe some day I'll be strong enough to read them...

My phone finds this time to start ringing at me. Grateful for the distraction, I check the caller ID and see that it's a blocked number. I stare at the piles of photos and poems and figure a blocked number is better than specific memories.

"Hello?" I squeak out.

Silence answers me.

"Hello? Is anyone there?" I'm pleased my voice sounds stronger, and yet no one answers me.

"Well that was a wasted distraction!" I say into the phone, cutting off the call as quickly as possible. Just when I could have used one, too.

"Okay...Emma," I say at my reflection in the mirror. "Put on your big girl panties and get this room packed up. You have a whole damn house to do and wallowing over memories isn't going to make this go any faster...or easier for that matter." I square my shoulders. "So man up."

And I do just that.

~~~

At six o'clock I finally call it at day. My room is barebones, except for my furniture, which I now realize I'll have to hire moving guys to help bring down to the truck since it's just little old me here. Or maybe I could donate it? I make a point to call the Red Cross tomorrow...I know we have a donation store in Henderson Center...Maybe they do pick-up?

I was also able to set in on the guest bedroom, which was really pretty easy because there wasn't anything in it. Daisy slept there and was kind enough to empty it out herself.

Feeling fairly accomplished, I head downstairs to make myself some dinner.

God...How many times have I gone up and down these stairs in my life? I pause at the bottom, looking from the living room to the dining room. The sheer volume of stuff makes my stomach drop.

How am I going to get through all this?!

Feeling overwhelmed is actually a welcome sensation to feeling on the brink of a massive panic attack.

I head for the fridge and go about pouring myself a glass of wine.

And then, on a burst of inspiration, I go to the "junk drawer" in the kitchen island and pull out the sticky notes and a pen. I figure since I'm riding the "fairly accomplished," wave I may as well stick with it all the way out. I start in the living room, placing a sticky note with a giant X on all the pieces of furniture I won't be keeping. The furniture I am keeping I leave alone.

I go over the whole house (except my parents' room) and once I'm done, the grandfather clock is the only item not brandishing an X. I know their bedroom houses Mom's hope chest and roll-top desk, the only other items I wish to keep. I just can't bring myself to open their door yet.

I'm now grateful that I chose the smallest of the U-Hauls, because what I will actually be taking home is minimal at best.

I ease out onto the front porch, refreshed glass in hand, and watch the treetops dance in the wind.

I go to bed without dinner, my appetite having apparently been packed away with all my childhood memories.

~~~

I'm watching my mom run through the redwood forest, clutching something to her chest. I'm trying to keep up with her, but she's unnaturally fast. Since when was Mom such a great runner?

"Mom! Mom, what are you doing?! Come back!" The wind carries my voice away.

"Mom!"

Suddenly I'm up in the canopy of redwoods, looking down on her as she digs into the soil with her bare hands. The bundle she was carrying is lying at her side. I try squinting to see what it is but I'm too high up to get a clear picture.

"Mom!" I scream, hoping she will hear me.

"Leave it alone, Emma," Dad says. He's hanging from a tree branch, noose tightened around his neck like a perverse choker. His eyes are bulging from his face, a face that is so blue it may as well be black.

I recoil so quickly from his deformed figure that my foot slips from the branch I'm standing on and then I'm tumbling through the canopy of redwood branches, feeling them rip the skin from my bones. It hurts terribly, but what hurts more is the look of utter betrayal I see on my mom's face as she looks up and sees my dad hanging from the tree like a dead animal.

She barely registers me crashing to the ground, right on top of her little bundle…

~~~

The hot spray of water does nothing to scorch away the dream I just woke from. My dad's face…my mom's…I shudder. Even Eddy was drenched in my sweat.

"I think I need to drink more," I say to the empty bathroom.

I spend about ten minutes simply soaping down, trying not to remember how it felt to have my skin torn from my body.

What a twisted dream!

Finally I relinquish the shower even though I don't feel clean. There's nothing I can do about the dream, however, but continue packing up my parents' house. For the sake of my own sanity I should really start working into the night. At least if I don't sleep, I won't have horrifying nightmares…

I dress in jeans and a tee-shirt and head downstairs with determination like liquid iron coursing through my veins.

I don't even bother with coffee, but instead start tackling the living room with a verve I didn't think I could possess after having such a fitful night's sleep. Or perhaps it's just that that makes me work as fast as possible…The sooner I get out of this house, the sooner I return to a saner state.

I pull down books from the bookshelves that line the living room walls and place them delicately into boxes. My mother was an avid reader and has everything from Shakespeare to Jane Austen to Carol Goodman lining her walls. It really is a small library.

"We live by words, Emma. Remember that the next time you scoff at your english teacher for making you read Tess *of the d'Urbervilles…Which just happens to be a literary classic!" She'd shoved the book into my hands (because of course she'd had a copy) and gave my temple a small kiss.*

I hold a copy of *The Bell Jar* by Sylvia Plath and just stare at its worn cover. I picture Mom coming home after a long day at the hospital, throwing on her pajamas and cozying down into the chair in front of the window, content to read for hours. She was always buying new books, discovering new authors, and by the time I'd hit high school I was almost as enamored with the written word as she was...So long as it wasn't something I had to write a paper on, of course. The thought brings unwanted tears to my eyes because it's a good memory, Mom reading, one I will always be able to cherish. For so long I was so focused on her slow decline that I never thought to try and remember the good moments, and that alone makes me feel like a terrible daughter.

I examine *The Bell Jar.* Its spine is creased so intensely you almost can't make out the title of the book. *How many times had Mom read this?*

I scan the other books and can't help but notice that none of the others look as heavily used as this one. Mom obviously loved this book. I flip through the pages, not horribly shocked that certain words and phrases have been highlighted. Only a lover of the written word would do such a thing.

Instead of demoting it to a box, I place it next to me, giving it a small pat before I resume my exhumation of all her beloved books.

~~~

It takes me longer than expected to box up the library. It's after two when I finally have everything tucked away.

I check my phone for any messages and slump a little when I realize I have none. *Doesn't anyone wanna talk to me?*

"Stop your belly-aching, Emma. They know not to bother you right now."

Which reminds me…

"Oh crap. I need to call the Red Cross."

I open Safari on my phone and Google their number. I'm really glad I remembered because if they can't come pick all this stuff up, I'm gonna be paying through the nose for movers.

"Thank you for calling the Red Cross. My name's Irene. How can I help you?"

"Hi, Irene. I have a question." I look around at everything that needs to go and try not to sigh. "I have a house full of furniture and…stuff…that I'd like to donate—"

"Oh, how wonderful!" Her enthusiasm startles me. I didn't know the Red Cross was so hard-up for merchandise.

"Yes, well…I'm clearing out my parents' house and don't have much use for a lot of their stuff." I clear my throat. "The thing is…It's just me doing all this and I can't handle a lot of the furniture. Do you happen to pick up?"

"Of course we do, dear!"

"Oh, thank Christ!" I let it out before I know what I'm saying and I hear a hearty laugh from the other end of the line.

"Let's schedule a day and time and we will get it all taken care of for you."

I know I have at least two more days of packing ahead of me, so we set it up for Friday. That will give me a good three days to get everything sorted out.

"What is your name, dear? And I'll need your address as well."

"My name is Emma Bell-"

"Oh!" *Damnit all to hell.* "Are you Ron and Evelyn's daughter?! You moved to New York, right?"

I clear my throat. "Yes ma'am."

26

"Oh you poor dear! I'm so sorry about your mom…and your father, for that matter. They were such wonderful people."

"Yes, they were…"

"How are you holding up, Emma? Your mother was in my book club for years up until…" Her voice wanes, no doubt because no one wants to say, "Until she lost her marbles."

The lightbulb clicks on…Irene Walters. For all Mom talked about her, I've never met the woman. Another reason I'm a disgrace as a daughter.

"I'm doing okay, Irene. Thank you for asking. It's…been a difficult time." *How much more clichéd can I get?*

"Well, if you need anything, let me know." She rattles off her number which I don't write down because I'm not going to unload eight years of woes on a woman I've never actually met. So instead I try to make my voice as cheerful as possible.

"Thank you so much, Irene. You've just saved my life."

"Hey…That's what the Red Cross does, right?"

We click off and I feel like the lowest scum you could find at the bottom of the pond.

I plunk down into a chair, staring at nothing.

How do I not know my parents' friends?

How do I not know what Mom's favorite books were? How do I not know anything?!

"Because I'm a selfish brat, that's why," I say to a box of books. It doesn't disagree with me.

I'm tempted to pop a cork and go to town on some wine but that's not a constructive use of my time…And it's way too early. So I temper those feelings of scumminess and forge ahead. I still have almost a whole house to disassemble. I

27

shove the boxes of books aside and start on all the other trinkets that pepper the room.

I'm really digging into a display of war figurines (complements of Dad) when my phone pings me.

- You okay?!

God bless you Mia!

- Hey babe. I've been better. Plugging away!

- When are you coming home?!

- Possibly this weekend?! I have the Red Cross coming on Friday to pick up all the furniture.

- You're getting rid of it all?!?! WTF dude!?

I can't help but laugh. Leave it to fiery Mia.

- I have no use for this stuff babe. I'm keeping a few things though…antiques :)

- :((((It's your family's shitznit though…are you okay with that?

I pause as I consider my answer. I look around the room at everything modeling an X. A small amount of resolve settles in me when I realize that, yes, I am okay with it because the few items I didn't X are the ones I really want. I didn't think I would want *anything* from Eureka… But as it turns out, I'm not as know-it-all as I thought I was.

- I know what I want :)

- Okay…work quicker so you can get your ass home sooner!! xoxoxoxo

I smile as I send her a kissy face.

I bet Heidi uses kissy faces…

Before I chicken out I'm calling her number. Or what I assume is her number because I haven't called it in years.

It rings and rings and rings. There's no messaging system. And then it just clicks off.

My heart drops to the floor. *Did she just cut me off?*

Not that I can blame her...

"Emma! Seriously? You're just going to up and leave?! What about our plans for college?!"

"I have no reason to stay, Heidi!"

"Yes! Actually you do! What about your family? Bryan? Me?!"

"I...I just can't, Heidi. You don't understa "

"I fucking understand!"

I physically jerk remembering the door slamming after she'd left my bedroom. I'd watched her walk out into the redwood forest towards her car, feeling a hollowness form in my chest that I didn't think could get any worse until the day I told Bryan...

I let that memory dissolve into oblivion.

"Get back to work, Emma."

I move like an old lady. I set my phone down and head over to my father's relic of World War I. He was such a huge history buff...Something I'm certainly not. That didn't stop him from dragging me and Mom to every battlefield around the country. If I remember correctly those were actually some pretty fun road trips. Mom and Dad would crank up the music and sing along to the likes of The Beatles, The Who, The Rolling Stones...

It's no wonder I'm the only 26 year old at the office who can recite every Moody Blues song out there.

I pick up a figurine of a Bristol Type 22, a two-seater fighter plane the British used during the war. Its construction is delicate, like it may break if I handle it incorrectly. The details are quite impressive. I picture Dad sitting at the dining room table, shoulders hunched as he assembled all these little figurines, tapping his foot to whatever song was playing on the stereo.

I set the plane on top of Mom's book and head to said stereo. I could use some Moody Blues right about now.

I spend the rest of the afternoon packing up the living room, listening to oldies music, enjoying everything from The Rolling Stones to Cat Stevens. When I'm done it's after six, I'm starving, and my two souvenirs—Mom's book and Dad's airplane—are wrapped safely within some bubble wrap and tucked into the recesses of my suitcase.

"For someone who ran away from them, you sure are a sentimental sap, Emma," I say to the house as I make my way into the kitchen. I start pulling out the makings for a salad, my mind flashing from one memory to the next.

I pour myself a glass of wine from the bottle I opened last night, the voice of Van Morrison crooning about Tupelo honey.

"Bryan loved this song," I say to the refrigerator door. "He said it would be our first dance song at our wedding."

Maybe it's because I have one more room under my belt all packed up and ready to go, but I suddenly feel like I'm better able to think about him without feeling like my internals may explode.

"He said we'd go to the junior college first and get all our basic classes covered and then transfer to a four-year, allowing us to save money. Ever sensible." I snort.

"He said Heidi and I could live together because he had a sweet set-up at his parents' house and he, well, he had a first-class seat to my parents's breakdown..."

Both Heidi and Bryan did. I'd show up at one or the other's house, sobbing, complaining that Mom was on one of her rants about ghost babies and my dad was passed out drunk in the guest bedroom.

*Ghost babies…*I'd forgotten about that. She ranted about a lot of things in the two years before I fled, but the most prevalent had been about babies. I'd always known she wanted more kids after me and I'd assumed that it was this want that made these particular rants damn-near unbearable. But what if it had been something else..?

Had she known..?

"That's ridiculous, Emma. There's no way."

I chop up the last of the green onions and dump them into the mixing bowl. I pull the rotisserie chicken I haven't touched from the fridge and start pulling off strips of flesh, shredding them into my salad.

"Gotta have protein."

Van Morrison has morphed into Peter, Paul and Mary.

"If I had a hammer…" I smile briefly, then frown into my salad bowl. "Emma, aren't you at all concerned that you've spent the last ten minutes talking to yourself…like you expect someone to respond back?"

My gaze shifts to the window, where the trees stand silent this evening.

"It's a little disconcerting."

I've been in this house barely three days and I already feel like I'm going crazy because, vocal monologue aside, I think I see a figure standing in the hazy light amidst the redwoods. The morning fog never lifted and so the whole forest has been one silent cloud bank, muting anyone and everything, making me feel like I could be on Mars instead of the boondocks of Eureka.

But even through this haze it looks like a person leaning against one of the trees, looking at the house like they're trying to decide the best way to break in. My mind glimmers to my dream, watching Mom running through the forest, Dad hanging from the tree…

I abandon my chicken and fiercely rub my knuckles against my eyes, hoping this will clear the vision, literally and figuratively. I drop my hands and want to dance a small victory jig when I see that the space between the trees is vacated.

"Just a play of the light and the fog, Emma," I breathe.

"But it's still not a very good sign that you're seeing things now." *Kinda like Mom.* Leave it to my brain to mention that little factoid.

"It's confirmed. Daytime is waaaaay easier in this place then nighttime," I say as I warily eye the spot outside one more time.

I turn back to my salad and throw some dressing on it, mixing it with two big spoons my parents had since before I was born. I forgo a plate, however, electing to simply grab a fork from the drain rack and take my gigantic bowl of salad into the living room for some TV dinner time. I cut off The Animals as I do.

"House of the rising sun," I say to the silence. I survey my surroundings. "Seems appropriate."

I think I'm done talking to myself for the evening.

Chapter 4

I turn off the TV. The grandfather clock has just informed me that it's eleven o'clock, and for all intents and purposes I should be dog tired. Except I'm not.

I'm surprisingly awake and I know why.

For the past five hours, I've felt like someone's been watching me and it's totally fraying my nerves. I tried eating away said nerves, I tried drinking away said nerves and I tried every rom-com I could find to calm said nerves. Nerves are not calming.

I toss back a little more wine and make the injudicious decision to go sit out on the front deck. The least I could do is go up to the second story deck, but I find that if someone is spying on me, I want them to know that I'm not intimidated… even if I am.

I slip out into the cool night and sit on the top step of the porch.

"Why don't you just sit in one of the deck chairs, Emma?" Dad asks as I plunk my six year old bottom down on the top step.

"Because, Papa, I have to be ready for when the fairies come."

Dad chuckles. "Oh, I see. And what are the fairies coming for?"

"Me, of course!" I brandish my arms wide like I'm the most important thing in the world.

"Why would the fairies come for you?" (My adult brain now realizes how patient my dad was with me.)

"Because I'm awesome!" I bounce up and down, fairy wings flopping gleefully.

"That you are," Dad laughs. "But there's a problem." He pauses to sip his beer. "They would have to get through me first."

I sip my wine, letting the memory get carried away with the cool night air. I watch the moonlight play off the tops of the trees, mingling with the fog on the ground that has gratefully thinned out over the past few hours.

"I know someone's there," I call into the night. My voice echoes through the trees, like it's riding along the waves of mist like a surfer. I don't *really* know if someone's watching me, but hey, I have no neighbors to hear me so I may as well use my isolation as an advantage.

So it about makes me drop my glass when someone actually responds.

"You sure went to town on that bottle, Emma. New York's turned you into a party girl."

No. Freaking. Way.

I ease slowly from my step and watch as Heidi walks through the trees, like a folkloric creature rising from the brume. She hasn't changed one bit; from her shoulder length blonde hair to her long and lanky build, she is every inch the eighteen year old soccer captain I left behind eight years ago. The moonlight bounces off her hair, radiates from her sea green eyes. I bite back a sob. I didn't realize how much I've missed her until this very moment.

"I know you called me today. And yes…I ignored your call because I didn't want my first conversation with you after eight years to be over the phone."

She stops at the bottom of the stairs and looks up at me. The light coming through the open door bathes across her face and I'm instantly reminded of all the Pre-Raphaelite muses I studied in art history. She's neither smiling nor frowning, so I can't tell if the chip on her shoulder is as large as it was all those years ago.

"Do you wanna come in?" My voice breaks.

"Of course. Why the hell else would I be here?"

I'd forgotten that Heidi was never one to hold her tongue.

34

We enter the house and I watch closely as her pace slows while she looks around, an expression on her face I can't quite place. Whimsical? Haunting? Melancholy? It saddens me that I can't tell, because eight years ago I would have pinned it like a tail on the donkey.

"Jesus…Never thought I'd set foot in here again." She walks into the living room and shrugs off her jacket, tossing it into a chair like she's done so many times before, and flops onto the couch.

"Do…Do you want anything to drink? Wine? Water?"

"Wine, please."

Never mind that it's eleven o'clock at night. I scurry away like a loyal servant.

After I've given her a glass, she takes three bountiful gulps.

"Heidi…listen—"

"No. No, tonight I'm doing the talking, babe." She takes a big breath. "Yes, I've been sitting in my car watching this house pretty much all night…It was the only way I could get my thoughts in order. And yes…I was the one that called you, but I couldn't speak." She pauses. "When you left here I was so mad at you I couldn't see straight." She looks around the room. "We'd been through everything together, Emma…*everything.* First days of school, first graduations, first loves, first periods…I felt like you were abandoning me." I bite my lips together to prevent myself from either crying or speaking, I'm not sure which. "It took me years to finally understand why you left. Watching your mom go through what she was going through…Your dad…Bryan…Fuck, I can't imagine what those last two years of high school were like for you." She sips her wine. "I was only thinking of myself when you left." She looks me straight in the eye and I see something in hers soften. "And for that, Em, I'm so, so sorry."

35

An unladylike sob breaks from my chest as I launch myself across the couch and catch her in the biggest bear hug I can possibly muster. She wraps her slender arms around me and holds me back.

I don't trust myself to speak yet, so we just hug, letting the tension drain from the room.

After what feels like forever, we disengage and sit back, smiling at each other like not a day has passed. *That's true friendship.*

"Oh God, Heidi, you have no idea how much I've missed you."

"Ditto. These past eight years have really bit the big one." She takes a sip of her wine and settles back into the couch, eyeballing all the boxes strewn about the room. "I don't even know where to start."

"Let's start with this…How are you?"

She laughs, a sound that makes this whole trip worthwhile.

"I'm doing okay…I own my own business down in Old Town, actually. Always had a thing for advertising."

"Oh wow! That's amazing, Heidi!"

"What about you? Are you still in New York?" I'm so grateful there's no hostility in her voice that I could cry again.

"Yes. My apartment is about the size of my bedroom upstairs and it costs an arm and a leg, but luckily I make good money writing for a large pet product company."

"You always wanted to be a writer." She smiles at me. "I remember you making up those stories about us being fairies lost in the woods…Have you ever considered turning any of that into a real book?"

Why I'd never thought of that is beyond me. I mean, I majored in English with a minor in creative writing. I guess I was so happy on getting my job right out of college that I never let the ideas formulate.

"Honestly, no." I laugh. "But that doesn't mean I can't. It would make a pretty good children's novel actually…Something about always finding your way home…" My eyes travel around my house, a place that has grown so foreign to me that I can't even stay a few nights without having heinous nightmares.

"Em, I'm really sorry about your parents. When I'd heard that Evelyn had passed away, I knew you would come back. And I have to admit I was stupid excited about it. I've been checking on the house every day to see when you'd show up."

I huff. "It's a blessing that she's gone. She was so out of her mind she didn't even know who she was any more."

"How do you know?"

"Daisy—she was the live-in caretaker—would update me every week on Mom's diagnosis."

Heidi nods, not saying anything. I think it's because we're both thinking the exact same thought: *It should have been me taking care of Mom.* The scumminess resumes.

"I've been really selfish, haven't I?" This is the first time I've actually said the words out loud and something like grief mixed with relief breaks like a shattered glass inside me.

Heidi bobs her head back and forth, making her hair swing, twisting her mouth to the side in thought. "Yes and no. You did what you had to do for *you*, which is totally understandable. But yeah…Your mom was sick, Em. She needed you."

Hearing it honestly from my best friend makes it very real that I was not, after all, the world's greatest daughter. After leaving, I can only imagine what this house turned into. Mom loping around, muttering to herself as Dad retreated to

37

the guest bedroom to douse himself in rum, vodka…whatever was on tap for the day.

"Shit. I'm a terrible person." I chug a gulp of wine and try not to cry.

"Oh, please. No one—well, besides me and Bryan," she laughs, "—blamed you for leaving. Everyone said you'd never come out of this house alive if you'd've stayed."

"Really?" I snivel.

"Yes, really." Heidi smiles at me. "You had every right to leave…but maybe just not to stay away so long," she adds with a teasing smile.

I can't help but laugh.

"Duly noted. So, have you…Have you seen Bryan much?" I can't look in her eyes when I ask and it makes me feel like scum all over again.

She shakes her head. "Not often. He left after you left, saying he couldn't stay here without you. I thought for sure I'd never see him again, but he popped right back up about four years ago. Works as a tech guy for all the 'big' companies around here." She air quotes "big" because we both know Eureka isn't Silicon Valley.

I try to picture Bryan working on computers, but the image disappears before it even fully forms.

"Good for him," I manage.

There's no way I can pull one over on Heidi, though. She sets down her glass and takes my hand.

"Em, you've got to talk to him. He hasn't been right for eight freaking years. Only you have the power to fix that." Her sea green eyes bore into mine. I realize now just how much Heidi cared about Bryan, and to see him just as distraught as she was herself couldn't have been easy.

"You're right…and I will."

~~~

I wake up the next morning feeling lighter than I have in months. Or more like years. I roll onto my side, Eddy clutched to my chest, and see that the sun is trying to make a break through the clouds...Just one more reason to feel uplifted.

Heidi and I stayed up until three last night, just reminiscing and catching up. To fall right back into the friendship we had after so much strife is a blessing I'm not sure I deserve. She even said she would come over today and help with the packing!

The thought propels me out of bed and into the shower. I take a long time cleaning up, enjoying the feel of the water cascading down my body. Now that Heidi is back in my life, it feels like there's nothing I can't do...for the most part.

She's 100% right that I need to make it right with Bryan, but the mere thought of coming face to face with him sends my stomach into another stratosphere. He was always so...godly...with his perfectly chiseled features and muscular body...

"Why me?" I whisper into the silence of the darkened car.

My sixteen-year-old self still can't believe that the glorious Bryan Reyes has his head in my lap as we sit atop a look-out viewing the lights of Eureka below us. I'd never much ventured up into the likes of Kneeland, but I see now that if he really and truly wants me, this will become "our spot."

"What do you mean?" He snuggles his head against my stomach and looks up at me.

"Like...Why are we here?" I'm not sure what I expect to hear. Because you seem like an easy target? Because I'm crazy? Because I'm horny? *So his answer kind of jars me.*

39

"I don't know," he says as he looks out the windshield into a night so clear you can see the Milky Way. "It just feels right."

I turn off the shower and grab my towel, willing that memory to wash down the drain. Of course, now that I've thought it, I can't *un*-think it.

"Damn memories," I growl. But I refuse to be in a bad mood today. Heidi is coming over and that's all that matters.

I dress quickly and head down to the kitchen to make a pot of coffee. I now wish I had some donuts or bagels or something to give her as a thank you for helping me. Packing will go ten times faster with a second hand…meaning I can leave sooner…

The thought is oddly saddening.

I shake it off and busy myself around the kitchen. I pull out some strawberries and grapes, making a pretty little arrangement on one of Mom's serving platters. I grab some mugs and set them out alongside some creamer and sugar. Both Heidi and I like to disguise our coffee.

I hear her car pull up the driveway and go to stand on the front porch to welcome her.

"Good morning, sunshine!" She yells through the open window. She hops out and swaggers to the trunk of her car, where she starts pulling out stacks of boxes. "I wasn't sure if you needed these, but I figured you can never have too many boxes."

We kiss cheeks as we head back inside. She dumps her load on the living room couch with a little huff.

"Oh my God, you made coffee! Thank you!" She hurries to the kitchen like the coffee may disappear at any moment. I'm laughing as I follow behind her, remembering that Heidi was never much of a morning person.

"So what are we getting started on today?" She asks as she dumps cream and sugar into her mug. I follow suit.

"I was gonna tackle the dining room and kitchen today. I can't really pack everything up because I still need to eat, but I figured since they had so much crap down here it may go faster with two people."

"Sounds good to me." She pauses to sip her coffee. "Have you packed up their room yet? Yours?"

"I've done mine...Which was an interesting adventure," I add dryly. "And for whatever reason, I wanna leave their room for last." It's a queer conviction, but I feel like I'll be paying tribute by saving their bedroom for the last and final clear-out. "Actually." I pause, looking around at all the X's bedecking the room. "Would you perhaps want some of this furniture? The ones with X's, I'm donating to the Red Cross."

"Wow...Really?! Shit. That's really nice." She regards the china cabinet. "I've always wanted one of these." She smiles over at me.

"It's yours." I go and remove the X. "If you see anything else, just remove the sticky note." It feels somehow appropriate that some of my parents' furniture will be going to Heidi. She was like a daughter to them, after all.

With coffee in hand, we start assembling boxes. I turn on the stereo and we sing along with The Monkees about being a believer.

~~~

"I can't believe how much stuff your parents had, babe." Heidi is standing in the middle of the dining room, surrounded by boxes that are stuffed to the gills with plates, pots, silverware, and anything else I won't be using for the next few

41

days. It took us all day to get the kitchen and dining room put away…If she hadn't been here, I would have been up to my eyeballs in frustration.

"Yeah, no kidding," I say as I swipe my arm across my sweaty brow. *I think I need another shower.* "Thank you so much for being here, Heidi. You made this sooooooo much more enjoyable."

She laughs, "Well…I do have one stipulation for my efforts today." She gives me a sly smile.

"Oh? And what would that be?"

"We're going out tonight."

I laugh. "Seriously? I can't go out tonight. I've got way too much to take care of around here."

"I'm here now. No you don't." She bats her eyelashes at me, making me laugh harder. "Oh, come on! It'll be fun! We've never painted the town red together, dude! That's, like, a staple as far as friendships go."

She has a point. I glance at the clock. It's already four o'clock.

"Okay, how about this," I say as I wade through the sea of boxes. "I need to shower because I smell like an old sock." She laughs. "But if you're willing to come get me, since all I have is the U-Haul, I'll go out tonight." A wink of excitement forms in my chest. *I get to go out with Heidi!*

"You got it!" She gives my butt a slap. "I'll be back in a few hours."

She gives me a fierce hug and waltzes out the door. I watch her car drive down the driveway and when she sticks her arm out the window and waves, I feel like my heart may burst.

I wave until I can't see her taillights anymore.

Even with the music on, the house feels strangely empty without her bold presence. I turn the stereo up so I can hear it from upstairs and head towards my bathroom.

I'm surprised at how sweaty I actually am. When the sun came out today, the house heated up about twenty degrees, reminding me that no air conditioning may not be a great selling point when this house goes on the market. But then again, Eureka rarely needs air conditioning.

I delight in my second shower of the day, taking the time to shave my legs and armpits. I can't very well look and feel like a woman if I look and feel like a yeti. I didn't exactly bring clothes to go out in because I didn't really think that was even a possibility. But on a last-minute whim, I pulled on my favorite pair of jeans, a designer splurge to celebrate my job out of college, and a cute teal halter top that accentuates my shoulders and back. I've worn this outfit before, so I know I at least look decent.

I blow-dry my hair and sweep it up into a claw, pulling out a few tendrils to frame my face. And, for the first time in days, I apply a light coat of makeup.

I regard myself in the mirror and decide that I'm passable. I actually feel somewhat human. I send Heidi a silent thank you for coming up with this idea. Three days alone in a house that can only be deemed as haunted has left me wanting for human interaction. I grab my sandals and laptop and head downstairs. I still have over an hour before Heidi gets here, so I figure this is prime time to check my emails and make sure all my assignments are taken care of. I even turn off the radio so I can concentrate.

My inbox is flooded. I weed through all the junk mail, pausing on a few newsletters I actually enjoy. I have an email from my boss asking how I'm doing and I reply with a brief and polite response that everything is going as scheduled and that I should be back to the office early next week. I've just barely sent the email when she responds back:

Sounds great kiddo! And thank you again for getting those articles about our new toy line in before you left…saved us a lot of grief.

Glad you are surviving! I've kept your plate bare until you return, so don't worry about work. Get home soon!

xoxoxo S

    I smile.
    It's like working with a family…Well, not my family, per se, but a well-adjusted family. And leave it to New Yorkers to never stop working. It's gotta be almost eight o'clock there and Sam is still at her computer!
    I plunk around on the internet, checking all the social media garbage that I've become inadvertently addicted to. If I didn't have to be on the likes of Facebook and Instagram and Twitter, I wouldn't be, but because I run all the posts for the company I work for, I have to stay on top of what's trending. Luckily, a co-worker is covering for me this week, because I don't think I could find the inspiration to be witty or creative.
    And, well, if I'm being honest here, social media has allowed me to keep tabs on all the people I left behind, namely Heidi and Bryan. It kind of makes me feel like a stalker, but my curiosity always wins out. For instance, I knew Heidi owned her own company, but I didn't want to seem like the pathetic loser who shadows her former BFF on Facebook. And much to my disgruntlement, Bryan hasn't been active on any kind of social media network for years, so I've been basically blind to his enterprises.
    I close my laptop just as I hear Heidi's car coming up the driveway. I grab my purse and jacket and step out onto the porch just as she's pulling up.

She whistles from her open window. "Damn, Em! I hate to admit it but New York living has agreed with you!"

"Oh hush!" I laugh as I lock the front door and skip down the steps to her car.

"Seriously, dude…" She waggles her eyebrows at me, making me laugh harder.

"You're no slouch there either, girl," I say, eyeing her long body up and down. She looks amazing in her black leggings and scoop neck sweater, showing off just the right amount of cleavage to be alluring. Throw in the knee high boots and you've got a bar fight waiting to happen.

We roll away from the house and it instantly feels like a weight's being lifted off of my chest. I crack the window and let the fresh air blow into my face, oxygenating me much like a Venturi mask might. I hadn't realized how oppressed I've felt since I'd gotten here, the weight of all those memories crashing down on me like a tidal wave. Sure, some of those memories aren't bad (hell, they could really be considered pleasant), but then to realize how it all turned out…I think that's what bogs me down the most.

The memory of my dream flits through my brain.

"Hey, Heidi…Did you ever see my dad? I mean…before he passed away, obviously."

She turns down the radio and glances over at me.

"On occasion. I'd usually see him at the supermarket. It was pretty obvious he was wasted most of the time." She gives me a sad smile. "Sorry."

"Don't be. I'm sure he was. It's just…Did he ever seem, I dunno, depressed or anything?"

"Well, Em…He was a drunk. I'm sure he wasn't skipping in circles and making daisy chains."

45

The image makes me laugh because it's so unlike my father.

"What I mean is...Did he seem, I dunno, suicidal?"

"Suicidal? Really?"

"It's just...I had this dream." I describe the dream to her as she drives. She listens intently, just like she always did when I'd come over after the latest philippic from Mom. When I finish she doesn't say anything for a few minutes. She just chews on her bottom lip and navigates the car through the streets of Eureka. I just now realize I have no idea where we're going.

"Damn, Em. Were you able to see what it was that your mom was carrying?"

"Nope."

"I mean...I hate to say it, but your dad was always kinda on the back burner when compared to your mom. No one ever really talked about his condition. All anyone ever talked about was Evelyn and how crazy she'd become."

"I know." The thought grieves me. "I mean...He died of alcohol poisoning. What if it was intentional?"

"I dunno babe." Heidi reaches over and pats my leg. "But I'm sure he's at rest now."

I nod because I can neither confirm nor deny her statement.

We're in Old Town, the historical portion of Eureka where all the local shops and restaurants reside. Seeing the gazebo with the flowing water fountain and all the Victorian architecture literally jars me. I'm pleasantly surprised this portion of town hasn't gone completely down the drain.

"Where are we going?" I ask.

"The local watering hole." Heidi laughs. "I'm not sure why it's such a popular hangout, but it is." She parks the car along the street and looks over at me. "You ready for this?"

46

I heave a sigh. "As ready as I'll ever be."

We exit the car, the breeze off the bay caressing my bare arms and back like a lover would. It smells of salt and fish and drives my memory back to when I'd come here shopping with my parents.

"Emma! Don't get too close to the water, sweetie," Mom says as she locks hands with Dad and they start a slow walk down the street.

My seven-year-old self abandons the magical water fountain, runs up and grabs Dad's hand.

"Can we go to the toy store? Please?!"

He laughs. "Maybe after we run our errands, kiddo. Mom's on a mission."

"I need a chest to hold all my crafts. I'm tired of it littering the dining room table."

"Yes, dear."

That was the day Mom bought the hope chest, one of the three items I'll be keeping for myself. I'd always loved the filigree tracery decorating the lid. It re-minded me of something a princess or a fairy would have had, thus my fondness for it.

"Alrighty, girlfriend. Let's get our drink on!" Heidi's standing in front of a door to an establishment that sits on the corner of one of the side streets. I see an ocean of bodies through the darkened windows, laugher and music permeating the evening air.

I square my shoulders. "Let's do this."

Chapter 5

When we enter the bar, I feel like every set of eyes land on us. I mean, really, I'm not terribly surprised because Heidi can turn the head of a blind man but it's oddly unsettling to feel like I'm on display.

Maybe I shouldn't have worn this top…

"You're the fresh new toy, Em," Heidi yells over the music. "People are gonna stare."

I give her a watery smile as she grabs my arm and starts elbowing her way up to the bar. I keep my eyes averted to the ground.

One would think that living in New York would turn me into a huge party animal, but the fact of the matter is that I'm just not. I prefer small, intimate get-togethers as opposed to a large, booming crowd. Sure, Mia and I would go out for cocktails, but it was always to some secret hole-in-the-wall restaurant with little-to-no traffic…Which is hard to find in New York. A bar hopper I am not.

"What would you like, Em?"

"Uh, I guess a glass of red wine." Nor am I adventurous.

She grabs the bartender's attention easily enough and shouts our order. Then she turns to me with a wicked smile. "I'm making sure that we have to Uber our asses home tonight."

This makes me laugh. I have no doubt about that.

The bartender brings us our drinks—*four* glasses of wine?!—and Heidi gives him her card to hold our tab.

"Drinks are on me tonight, babe. In celebration of you finally coming home!" She hands me two glasses of wine. Looks like I'm double-fisting for the evening.

We vacate the bar and head towards the back of the room in search of an empty table. I'm amazed that so many people are here, considering it's a Wednesday night and it's not even 6:30. We do manage to find a little corner table and swoop down on it like a couple of falcons.

I've managed to keep my head down, but now that we're seated I have nothing to do but scrutinize the crowd. If I'm expecting to see anyone I know, I'm sorely disappointed. The crowd is younger, college kids, probably from Humboldt State in the sister town of Arcata. The girls all look like bimbos and the boys all look like idiots.

"Since it's summer, the crowd is a little younger than it normally is," Heidi explains. "I'm sure some old-timers like us will show up eventually...After the kids have been put to bed," she laughs.

"Hey...So speaking of, are you seeing anyone right now?" I'm not sure how we didn't cover our love lives last night.

"Nah," she says flippantly, waving a dismissive hand in the air. "I've got my business to focus on. Work is a decent enough aphrodisiac for me," she says with a wink. "What about you?"

"Good grief, no!" I laugh. "I can barely keep my houseplants alive, much less a relationship."

"Surely you've had to have dated someone?" We both eyeball a group of guys who keep leering at us. "Jesus, it's like watching wolves descend on the flock."

"No kidding," I laugh. "My friend Mia tried to set me up with her cousin, but I just wasn't that interested."

"That's it? What do you do, walk around with a bag over your head all day?"

I chuckle. "I could say the same about you."

49

"Hey there, ladies. Having a nice evening?" One of the wolves has separated from his pack, no doubt sniffing out if we are good enough stock. He's not a bad-looking guy with his tall build and blonde hair, but the way he asks our breasts how our evening is rates him at about a two.

"It's fine, thank you. Just catching up with a dear friend who's visiting from out of town." Heidi's voice is cool and unimpressed. I wish I had the nerve to rebuke someone so easily. I'm always afraid of hurting their feelings. This trait of mine has lead me to some pretty awkward cocktails.

"Care if we join you? I'd love to get to know your friend." He looks me up and down like I'm his dinner.

"Yes, I do care. Now run along, little boy." Heidi flutters her hand at him and turns back to me, completely dismissing him. If his shocked expression is any indication, I'd say he doesn't get shot down all that often.

We hear a muttered "bitch" and then he retreats back to his pack, no doubt to find some other poor girl to lick his wounds.

I clink my glass against hers as I say, "That was impressive."

She gives me a rueful smile as she asks, "So what are we packing up tomorrow, babe?"

I give her a startled look. "Really? You wanna keep helping me?"

"Hell yeah, I do! Otherwise I won't get to see you! Plus, it's kinda fun going through all their stuff...Brings back a lot of memories."

"It really does," I think about Mom and her "ghost babies." Despite the stuffy air, I shiver. "Hey, I have a question...Do you ever remember me complaining about Mom ranting about ghost babies?"

"Oh my God, do I ever! Scared the crap outta me, honestly." She scrunches up her face like she's trying to recall a difficult memory. "When did that start?"

"Around 2008-ish...My junior year," I say into my drink.

"Yes, that's right."

I lean my head closer to hers so I don't have to yell this next part. "It was also around the time of the abortion…What if she somehow found out?"

Heidi starts back, no doubt shocked that I would bring up the very thing that made me run in the first place. She looks around the room, eyes wide, probably wondering if anyone had heard me.

"You know what? Let's go outside for a little more privacy." She pats my leg as she stands. We grab our glasses and shoulder our way through the crowd, ignoring the sidelong glances from practically every male in the room. Luckily none of them advance on us. Maybe they can tell not to disturb two women who clearly have something to discuss.

There aren't many people out on the little patio attached to the bar. It's a cute little place, with lights strung up along the lattice work that hangs over the sets of tables and chairs. The music from inside is being pumped out through a single speaker attached to the side of the building, but the volume is much lower, making it easier for talking.

Heidi and I sit in chairs shoved up against the back fence, giving us ample privacy.

"Okay…Now, *what* are you talking about?!"

"I was thinking about it yesterday. Like, it *just* occurred to me that it was around the time I had the abortion that Mom really went off the deep end. Is it possible that she knew?"

"No. No, there's no way." Heidi shakes her head adamantly. "We went to that clinic in Garberville, babe. There's no way anyone could have found out. It's, like, an hour away from here."

"I suppose…But isn't it just a weird coincidence that I go through that horrible ordeal around the time Mom starts talking about babies?"

51

"Yes," Heidi says slowly, sipping her wine. "Yes…It is weird. We were so careful though…"

I huff and take a generous gulp of wine. "I dunno…Maybe I'm trying to make something out of nothing."

"…Or not." Heidi looks over at a couple locked in a passionate embrace, not really seeing them. "Maybe there's something there…something in the house that would confirm or deny this theory…"

I consider this. *Maybe there is.*

"If there is, I have no doubt it would be in their bedroom, which actually turned out to be Mom's because Dad ended up sleeping in the guest room up until he passed away."

"Well…Isn't that the only room that needs to be packed up? We could start tomorrow."

"God…Do I even want to know?!" I give a nervous laugh because, really, if I find out that Mom knew about my abortion and it drove her to insanity, I will never forgive myself. What if she told Dad and that caused his drinking problem?!

"Okay…We can address all this crap tomorrow, Emma," Heidi says as she leans over to wrap an arm around my shoulders. "For tonight, we are going to have fun and be careless, got it?"

I laugh, trying my hardest to shake off the scum. "Sounds like a plan." The clink of our glasses seals the deal.

~~~

We've just finished off our second glass of wine and are snaking our way up to the bar. Heidi was right; many of the college kids have thinned out to a more mature crowd.

"OH. MY. GOD!" Someone exclaims from behind me. "Emma! Emma Bell!" I turn around and come face to face with Stephanie Crnich, one of my good friends who, surprise surprise, I'd lost all contact with after high school.

"Oh my God! Steph!" I'm being wrapped into a gigantic hug before I can take my next breath.

"You look amazing, Emma! How are you? What have you been up to? Oh my God, I'm so sorry to hear about your mom!" The barrage of questions throws me off for a second. Or maybe it's the wine.

"I don't even know where to begin," I laugh.

"See, Steph...I told you I'd get her out!" Heidi sidles up next to us and places a glass of wine in my hand.

"You...You planned this?" I ask incredulously.

"Of course! How the hell else would you get reacquainted with everyone?" Heidi proudly sips her own glass, nearly dribbling it down her sweater for how wide she's smiling.

"You sneaky little brat!" I laugh as I swat her arm.

"Come on, then! We've got a ton of catching up to do!" Stephanie is pulling me over to a table that holds her coat. A man's seated there as well, who smiles and stands as we approach.

"Emma," Stephanie grins, "I'd like you to meet my husband Ryan. Babe, this is Emma, the show-stopper of high school."

I roll my eyes at her but smile warmly as I shake Ryan's hand.

"It's nice to meet you, Emma. Steph's said so many nice things about you over the years." He pauses and clears his throat. "I'm sorry to hear about your parents."

I'm just gonna have to get used to people saying that to me.

As we settle into our seats, a very fervent thought forms: If Heidi invited our friends from high school, then wouldn't it stand to reason she's also invited Bryan? Would he even want to come?

"Emma! Earth to Emma!" Steph's laughing as she waves a manicured hand in my face. "Good Lord, where did you go just then?"

"I…" I glance over at Heidi and I can tell she knows exactly where my thoughts were. Her expression to the untrained eye, however, leaves everything to the imagination. "Sorry, Steph…Sometimes I kinda get lost in my thoughts."

"Ha! Don't we all! So tell me everything! How's New York? How long are you in town for?"

We spend the next hour catching up and while it's wonderful to see Steph and to know that she's doing so well (a husband and two kids will do that to a person), I can't help but feel my eyes wander the room, constantly looking for the one person I do and don't want to see the most. A number of old friends show up, turning the bar into a makeshift reunion party. As the evening progresses, I get more and more anxious that Bryan *won't* show up, which just goes to show how much I *want* him to show up. And this realization does all kinds of trouble to my now alcohol-infused brain.

"I think it's time I whipped your butt at some pool, Emma," Kyle says. He was once Heidi's boyfriend and it's good to see that their break-up our senior year hasn't effected their friendship.

"I say you're on. Although, I should warn you that I've been practicing over the years." I laugh as we stand and make our way to the pool tables towards the back of the bar. Kyle's family was pretty wealthy, hence the game room we would flock to on the weekends, spending hours playing darts and pool and drinking Zima beer. We thought we were so cool back then…

"You rack, I'll break," I order. I think the wine has lowered my inhibitions because rarely do I ever order people around.

"Listen to you, all big-city girl!" Steph teases as she sits onto Ryan's lap. I notice they've become increasingly more touchy-feely as the evening advances and I have to wonder if baby number three may be conceived in the bathroom stall. The thought makes me laugh.

"What's so funny?" Heidi asks as she hands me a pool stick.

"Random thought, is all."

"Hey, Em, can I just say it's so good to see you having fun and laughing," Heidi says as she links her arm with mine and leans into me. "I had a feeling you would need this. I mean, you're still Emma, but you just seem, I dunno…a little sadder."

I consider her words as I watch Kyle rack up the balls. It's true, after all. If I'm being honest with myself, I'd say I haven't been myself since before the abortion. The whole experience soured me, made me feel less than human, more like a ghost.

"It's true," I say to her. "I have been sad, for a long time actually, but I think coming back here, however hard it is, will help put some of the past to rest."

"Agreed."

My body goes completely still. My heart flutters, falls to my feet, jumps right back up into my chest and starts a hammer that I'm sure the whole room can hear, even over the bass of the music.

Heidi disengages from my arm, giving me a small smile. I really wish she would stay at my side because I suddenly feel like vertigo is taking over my body.

The one voice I've been dreaming of and dreading to hear is standing right behind me. I can practically feel the heat coming from his body. I close my eyes as an onslaught of memories cannonade my mind, making me even dizzier than I already was.

Breathe, Emma. You knew it was coming.

But did I? Did I really think he would show up tonight…after everything I'd put him through?

I open my eyes and turn in a slow circle. I'm very aware that everyone is looking at me, no doubt waiting for me to pass out. Bryan did always have that effect on me.

I come face-to-face with his chest. One little twitch of my neck will bring me eye-to-eye with him, but I find that I can't do that…not yet. I examine the emblem on his shirt, watching the rise and fall of his chest as he breathes. I remember running my hands up and down that chest, feeling his heartbeat…

We've just made love, yet again, and now we're lying in bed together.

My seventeen-year-old self has her head resting on his chest as he gently strokes my back. Postcoital lethargy radiates up and down my body, making me feel sensitive to even the smallest of sounds, the smallest of vibrations.

I press my ear into his chest, listening to his heart. This heart that loves me so, so much. This heart that has to keep on beating for as long as my heart beats because otherwise I don't think I could live.

I feel a small tear run down my cheek at the thought of losing Bryan. I can't lose him. I won't.

I raise my head and look into his beautiful eyes.

"I love you."

"I love you too, Em."

Something akin to despair breaks inside me because, really, that's exactly what I did…I did lose him. And it was all my own doing. It was all my fault.

What do I expect to see when I look up? An expression of anger? Hate? Betrayal? I can't stare at his shirt forever, though. My head feels uncommonly heavy as I lift my chin to find Bryans's eyes.

If I'm expecting to see a broken man, I'm greatly mistaken. What stands before me reaffirms my thought that Bryan was always godly. His chest has filled out some, tapering down to a narrow waist and hips. His arms are tanned, toned, and I can see a peek of a tattoo sticking out the bottom of his shirt sleeve. *Bereaved men don't get tattoos, do they?*

His face is still that chiseled work of art I remember from my picture. Only now he looks more dignified. More mature.

And his eyes - *dear GOD I've forgotten how lovely they are* - are looking down at me with something in them that I can't recognize...or won't recognize.

"Hey there, Emma." His beautiful bass voice wraps around me like a cloak.

"Hi, Bryan." I turn a rich shade of crimson hearing my voice break.

Heidi, God love her, comes to my rescue.

"Bryan! You made it! Come on, dude, grab a seat!" She comes around and wraps an arm around his shoulders, guiding him around me so that I may find a minute to come back down to earth...Which doesn't happen because, like his voice, his cologne swaddles me and momentarily makes me feel like I'm going to float away.

His eyes don't leave mine until he's passed by me completely. I still have no idea what his eyes are telling me.

I watch as he greets everyone with a broad smile, doling out handshakes and hugs. I'm fleetingly disappointed that I did not receive such a greeting, but then again, I was the one who stomped on his heart eight years ago and didn't even look back to consider the devastation.

Some freaking fiancée I was...and daughter...and friend...

57

The sensation of scumminess threatens to overwhelm me.

Heidi comes to my side and bumps her hip into mine. "You knew it was going to happen eventually. At least here you have multiple buffers."

I give her an insipid smile. "I'm scum-"

"Well, come on, Emma! Let's get this game started!" Kyle breaks into my monologue of self-loathing.

"Yeah, show us what you've learned over there in the Big, Bad Apple!" Steph laughs. I inwardly cringe. *No need for reminders here, people!* My eyes skirt over Bryan, but his face is gratingly inexpressive. He just pulls on the neck of his beer, his eyes never leaving me. I literally have to shake myself to get my legs working again and I think I see a ghost of a smile cross his full lips.

"Okay then," I squeak out. I focus my energy on the pool table. I align the white cue ball at the apex of the triangle, line up my shot and dart my stick out in one swift motion. The audible crack of billiard balls brings a grin to my face. Kyle's eyebrows shoot up into his hairline and he whistles.

"Damn, Em...Nice break."

I'm pleased to see two stripes roll into the corner pockets.

"I told you I'd been practicing." *Thank God my voice sounds normal.*

"No shit," Steph laughs.

It's true, too. Not being a huge party animal but needing some kind of social interaction has led me to a number of establishments housing pool tables. I've found that the easiest way to engage people without actually having to engage them is by playing pool. The better I got, however, the more attention I received from the opposite sex...Something I wasn't looking for.

That's not the case right now. I can feel Bryan's eyes move with me as I meander around the table. It's oddly erotic.

Kyle and I banter back and forth, my sassiness returning with each sip of wine I have and each ball I sink. Before long I'm aiming for the eight ball and Kyle is huffing like a fractious child. When it sinks into the side pocket with a satisfying clunk, I raise my head and give him my best Devil-may-care smile.

"Rematch?" I ask.

Heidi and Stephanie bark with hysterics. From the corner of my eye I even see Bryan's shoulders shaking with suppressed laughter.

Kyle can't help but smile as he says, "No, thank you. I'd like to keep my manhood intact for the evening."

Ryan eases out of his chair and drapes an arm around Kyle's shoulders. "I'm buying you a drink." He side-glances at the numerous solids gracing the felt. "If I got fucked that hard, I'd need a drink afterwards anyways." I watch their retreating backs, not even bothering to hold in the snorts.

"Em, how you doing on your drink? Need a refill?" Heidi asks as she watches me finish off the last bit of my wine.

I hold the glass up and deliberate on my current state of inebriation. *Am I swaying? No. Am I slurring? No.*

"Sure," I say.

She grabs my glass just as Steph exclaims, "I'll join you! I need a refill myself."

And just like that, my two best friends are sauntering away, leaving me and Bryan in an awkward silence. I glance over at him and blush harder when I see he's still looking me over like he's trying to read between the lines. For all I know, he probably is. I grip my pool stick tighter, planting it firmly into the ground like my own personal pillar of strength. I'm ashamed to feel my palms grow sweaty. *How does he do it?*

He unfurls himself from his seat, stands, and walks right up to me, placing his hand on my cue. His cobalt eyes tunnel down at me, making my tongue stick to the roof of my mouth. My heart picks up its temperamental rhythm and I fear he will see it beating against my ribcage.

"Seems you've learned a thing or two since I tried to teach you." His voice is like velvet. "Care to make it interesting?"

"Huh?" *Why does my IQ drop twenty points when he's around?*

The corners of his mouth curl up, giving me a hint of that smile I've been dreaming about for eight years.

"You rack. I'll break," he says. *How long was he standing behind me?!* His hand leaves my stick, but not before his fingertips brush the top of my wrist. The sensation makes my core clench and my knees wobble.

"O-okay," is my pioneering answer.

I move on wooden legs as I gather up the balls and assemble them in the rack. I watch from the corner of my eye as Bryan goes to the wall of cues and starts searching for one that hasn't been beaten into the ground too hard. He finally settles on one to his liking, checking its straightness by rolling it along the top of the table, making sure it doesn't wobble. *Did he teach me that trick?* I want to say yes.

I place the rack in its appropriate spot, gingerly lifting it to reveal a tightly packed bundle of billiards.

"Very nice," he says, chalking up the tip of his cue.

"Who knew I could rack balls so well." Oh…good *grief!* I mentally slap my forehead with one hand as I slap my other mental hand over my mouth. *Did I really just say that?*

He bites his lips together to keep from smiling. No doubt because I don't deserve to be graced with one of his smiles. His eyes, however, are dancing. A very small victory for Team Emma.

"There's the Emma I know," he mumbles as he bends over to take his first shot.

I glance over and see Heidi and Steph watching us from the bar like they're in cahoots, which, based off the wide grins decorating their pretty faces, they must be. *Very sly, ladies.* I mentally roll my eyes.

The break of balls draws my attention back to the table. I watch as a stripe and a solid both glide into pockets. I guess it's anyones game now.

"Solids," Bryan says, claiming his preference. He lines up his next shot, his hands expertly handling the pool stick. I watch it slide in and out of his fingers and my mind goes to a place that is all but X-rated. I can't keep the blush down.

"So, Em, how's it feel to be back?" I silently commend Kyle for pulling my mind out of the gutter but his question makes Bryan's shoulders visibly tense. Does he think I'm back for good?

"It's...uh...It's strange...To say the least." We've already covered the death of both my parents earlier this evening, so there's no need to rehash that. What we haven't really covered is how I'm handling being back. "It feels..." *Honesty is key.* "Foreign. Driving here, being back with the redwoods, seeing the house and how completely warped it's become...It's like entering a different world."

Bryan misses a shot and curses under his breath. The tension around his mouth informs me he's not just annoyed at missing a shot.

I scan the table, examining all the angles, as Heidi and Steph come back with more wine. Steph hands me my glass and gently clinks hers with mine as she says, "It's not so horrible, coming back, is it? You get to see us, after all." It's meant to be a joke, but I can see Bryan's jaw twitching, an augury that he's agitated. I can't say I blame him.

I find his eyes as I say, "No...No, it's not so horrible."

~~~

The game is closer than I thought it would be but Bryan still manages to beat me. Our conversation changed from me being back to who's dating whom to, currently, what we should do next. It's not late, about nine o'clock, and Kyle's already proclaimed he's calling in sick tomorrow, as is Stephanie. Bryan hasn't said much the whole evening but now he decides to speak up.

"Why don't we head over to Myrtletown? There's a great dive bar we can go to. And I think they sell food, which is good because I'm starving."

I have to admit I'm not ready to call it a night either. I've played it right having one glass of water per one glass of wine, and while I irrefutably feel the effects of the alcohol, I'm in no way intoxicated. Plus, I'm also hungry.

"Let's do it!" Heidi proclaims. "However...I don't think any of us should drive. Steph, can you call an Uber while I close out my tab?" Steph nods and pulls out her phone as Heidi heads towards the bar. Kyle and Ryan are in a heated discussion about the San Fransisco Giants. It's just me and Bryan...again. He leans in closer to me, a cocky look on his face. His cologne all but makes me lightheaded. It's the same it was eight years ago, just as intoxicating now as it was then.

"I won the pool game."

"That's nothing new." I make myself laugh to cover up his effect on me.

"We had a bet, though."

"We...We did?"

"Yes, we did."

Care to make it interesting? I remember the question, but we never settled on how much to bet. I was still too flustered.

"We didn't bet anything, though." I can feel my heart starting to overuse itself again.

"*We* didn't…But I did." For the first time this evening he graces me with one of his smiles. I'm so awestruck by it's beauty, it takes me far too long to form my question.

"What did you bet?" I'm mortified my voice has gone up an octave.

His smile widens. "I bet that if I won I'd be the one taking you home tonight."

Chapter 6

The bar Bryan suggested is, indeed, a dive. But it's not as crowded as the last place we were at and it's a little quieter, easier to hold conversations. Not that I can really hold a conversation because my tongue is still tied up after hearing Bryan's proclamation. And, of course, he didn't elaborate. He just touched my shoulder, a gesture that sent my heart running out the door, and said he had to take a piss. The juxtaposition did manage to make me laugh, however shakily.

Now we're all seated at a round high-top table, drinks in place and an easy banter going on between Heidi and Steph concerning who was the better soccer player in high school.

"Clearly, it was me," Heidi says haughtily. "I *was* captain."

"Only because Couch Dellany had the hots for you," Stephanie laughs. It's true actually. It was a well known fact that Heidi could get away with murder during practice and Dellany would all but cut off his foot to protect her. Still…I'd say it's a toss-up as to who was better.

"Do you still play volleyball, Em? Dance?" Kyle asks, somewhat unexpectedly.

While Heidi and Steph were terrors on the soccer field, I was a terror on the court. Not only was I captain of the volleyball team, I was also captain of the dance team. We weren't exactly cheerleaders, but we'd perform for every football and basketball game. It made for a very busy school year.

"Not so much," I say, very aware of the heat coming off of Bryan, who chose to sit next to me. "I danced in college, but once I graduated, I didn't have the time." I twirl the stem of my wineglass between my fingers, remembering the anticipatory excitement before each game, feeling the adrenaline course through me with each perfect spike or pirouette. Nostalgia claws at my throat, so I take a hearty swallow of wine to wedge it down.

"And how was college for you?" Bryan's question silences the table. His jaw isn't twitching, but his eyes pierce mine and I feel that effect all the way down to my bone marrow.

"It was…okay…" I draw out the last word because I don't know what else to add. It's no secret that I planned my escape to New School College long before I told anyone I was leaving. The only people who actually know the real reason why I left are Bryan and Heidi. Everyone else just thinks I was trying to escape my parents' decline.

"Just okay?" Bryan's voice is almost mocking, flicking on a light of annoyance in my chest.

"It was your typical college experience."

"With what? Frat parties? Bar hopping? Come on, Emma. Tell us all about life in New York as a beautiful college student."

"Bryan…" Heidi half whispers. I know he's goading me, trying to get a reaction out of me. This knowledge doesn't stop my annoyance from flaming up into anger. My anger, however, isn't exactly justified. I left. I broke his heart. He has every right to push my buttons.

"No, Bryan," I say in my calmest voice, looking him dead in the eye even though it makes my stomach turn summersaults. "No parties. No bar hopping."

His jaw twitches but he doesn't say anything else. He takes a long draw from his beer and sets it back down with a little too much emphasis, jarring Steph's martini so that liquid spills over the table.

"Bryan, stop being an asshole," Kyle laughs, trying to lighten the mood. I implore him to stop speaking, but I'm graced with no such decorum. "You can't really blame Emma for escaping her parents. Shit, if anyone knew what she was going through it would be you, right?"

I actually wince. *Oh, the humanity.*

"Oh yeah," Bryan laughs as he stands from his chair. "Oh. Yeah. I knew every sordid detail. Every skeleton in the closet. Isn't that right, Emma?"

"Bryan," Heidi says, a little more loudly.

"No, Heidi," he snaps at her. "It's about fucking time I got to say my piece."
With that he grabs my arm and starts pulling me towards the door. I damn near
trip over my own feet.

"Wh…What are you doing?!" I gasp. I look back and see Heidi standing
from her seat but Bryan has already beaten her to the punch.

"Heidi, NO!" That one syllable stops her in her tracks and effectively brings
everyones attention towards us. He's completely unaffected by it while my face
burns with the fire of a thousand suns. I can't say I'm terribly surprised though…I
knew I had this coming to me. I knew it the day I left him.

Bryan throws open the front door and storms us out into the night. Even in
his anger, though, I notice that his grip on my arm is gentle. That simple fact
brings tears to my eyes. Bryan would never hurt me.

It's a clear night, much like the ones he and I would experience up on Kneeland, with the stars blinking down at us and the night air caressing our bodies…

He releases my arm but keeps on walking. I'm unsure if I should follow him,
but he solves that problem by doubling back and stomping towards me like a deranged animal.

"Emma—" He cuts off and turns around, walking away again. He runs his
hands through his hair like he's trying to rip it from its roots. He turns around and
comes at me again.

"Emma, goddamnit—"

"Bryan, please…I know you're angry with me—"

I don't finish my sentence because his hands have found my face and his lips
have found my mouth.

It's like the universe has exploded in one galactic firework. Stars shoot past
my eyes, moons collide, suns orbit and dance with each other in a seductive tan-
go…And yet nothing is more spectacular than feeling his mouth on mine. His lips

are soft and warm, taking me back to all those kisses we stole from one another... God, there must have been thousands! Bryan was always a good kisser, but the man who's attached to my face now is a whole other ballgame. His lips seem to take what they want. These are not the lips of a boy in love who thinks he has all the time in the world, but lips of a man who's run out of time; they exude desperation of trying to bring something back and never let it go. The only reason I know this is because my lips are telling the same story.

I twine my arms around his shoulders and press my body into his, which awards me with a deep groan. His hands slide through my hair, drawing my face impossibly close as our tongues blend together. I don't feel the cold of the breeze, I don't hear the sound of the cars passing by...All I have is Bryan. Even the ground seems to drop away, leaving me suspended in his arms.

We don't disengage from one another until an exorbitantly loud man stumbles through the front door of the bar, cursing about something I can't quite make out because all I can hear is our ragged breathing.

Bryan holds my face as he looks into my eyes. "I've been wanting that for eight years."

Tears threaten to make an ugly entrance, so I gulp them back and try to form words.

"Bryan, I know I have a lot of explaining to do. And I owe you about a thousand apologies, but..." My eyes travel to his mouth, wanting nothing more than to feel those lips on mine again.

"Yes, you do," he whispers. "But this is not the place for that." He kisses the tip of my nose. "Stay here. I'm going to get your purse and then, like I said, I'm taking you home."

~~~

I shot Heidi a text on the way home telling her that I'm fine and I'd see her in the morning for more packing. She replied right away that she was Uber-ing home herself and wants to hear every dirty detail over coffee tomorrow.

Bryan said very little as he navigated his car through the redwoods towards my house, giving me ample time to figure out what the hell I'd say to him. And allowing me to count the ways The Equals want their baby to come back...

Does Bryan want his baby to come back?

Maybe I was still in shock from the nights outcome, because all I could think about until we pulled up to my house was how a song like that would rank number thirty-two on the Top 40 list while that crappy version from 1977 got number one. I guess people in 1968 didn't appreciate the artistry behind exquisite harmony.

Now, as I grab us a couple glasses of water after we've come inside, I find that that time was sorely wasted. I have no idea how to even begin my redemption.

I hand him his glass and ease onto the couch. I watch him closely as he takes in all the boxes. He was just as much a part of this house as Heidi was, after all.

"I'm not sure you ever knew, but I came to visit your parents a few times," he says.

This surprises me...And also makes the scumminess come back in droves. Even my ex-boyfriend had come to my parents' aide while I'd been conveniently tucked away on the other side of the county.

"I'm sure they really appreciated that," I say softly.

"They did," is all he says.

I take a sip of my water, not just to wet my palate but to also bide my time because I have a lot of apologizing to do.

"Bryan," I start. His blue eyes seem to look into my soul. "I'm so, so sorry for what I did to you. I've been...pretty selfish over the years. I didn't think about anyone but myself..." I bite my lips together to keep from crying. My mind takes me to that day, just after we'd graduated, when I dropped the bomb on him...

"I'm moving to New York, Bryan." I can picture my eighteen-year-old self standing like a wooden doll amongst the redwood trees, feeling like I myself may grow roots and then I'll be stuck here forever.

"You're what? No way." He laughs, obviously thinking I'm making a joke.

"Yes," I say softly, maybe so the trees won't witness my betrayal. "I applied to the New School College in New York. I was accepted and I'm moving out there tomorrow." No need to sugarcoat it...The deed's been done.

Bryan's brow furrows, confusion blemishing his usually handsome face.

"But...but...what about..." I watch as his jaw starts twitching. "You can't just... What?!" He starts pacing in front of me like a caged animal. And I guess he is; I'm the one who put him in this cage.

"Bryan," I try to soothe. "After what happened last year, and with my parents, I just can't stay here anymore."

"Oh God, Emma, please." Tears brim his eyes as he grabs my hands in his. "I know last year was terrible. I know how much the abortion destroyed you. But, babe, we're a team...We've been a team forever. We can get through anything-"

"No, Bryan," I cut him off as I detach my hands from his. "No. I'm...I'm not right... anymore. I can't stay here and live with what I did. I can't watch my mom—" A sob breaks loose. "—or my dad..." I let a tear fall because all my energy is going into not falling into Bryan's arms and taking it all back.

I take off the engagement ring and place it in his hands.

"I'm so sorry, Bryan...But I just can't."

I run all the way home listening to him call my name.

"Emma?" Bryan's hand comes to a rest on my shoulder, effectively pulling me back from that harrowing day. If I remember correctly, I'd locked myself in my room and cried until I passed out.

"Sorry," I say with a small smile. "Just going down memory lane."

"What were you remembering?"

"The day I told you I was leaving," I say into my glass. "I don't think I'll ever be able to apologize enough for what I did to you."

"Yeah, well..." He sits back into the couch and throws an arm behind his head. "Let's just say that day doesn't exactly make my list of Top Ten Days."

"Nor mine."

"Emma." Bryan leans forward so his arms are resting on his knees. "Do you think...that if we hadn't gotten pregnant our junior year and if...you hadn't nearly died from the abortion...well." He looks down at his hands. "Do you think you would have stayed? Even despite your parents?"

"I would have stayed," I tell him. It's true, after all. Something had gone wrong with the surgical abortion, which had caused septic shock, a medical emergency I wouldn't wish on anyone. I pulled through well enough, but the damage had already been done. Not only did I resent myself for killing a living being, I also resented that very being for almost killing me. There are no words to describe how messed up I was from that. Messed up enough to deceive everyone I loved, I guess.

"I was really twisted after that, Bryan. I put on a brave face and pretended like everything was okay, but really...I had reached my tipping point." I draw my knees up to my chest, making myself as small as I feel. "I lied to everyone I loved. I let you all believe I was staying, that everything was okay, that I'd watch after my mom and dad. I was just so disappointed in myself..." My voice trails off as I stare out the window.

70

"I saw your mom that day." Bryan's staring into the fireplace, a nostalgic look on his face. "After you ran away from me, I basically collapsed to the ground. I couldn't move. I was so heartbroken that I'd wished the ground would open up and swallow me." He gives a humorless laugh. "So imagine my surprise when I look up and see your mom walking through the woods. I thought she was coming to see me, but she didn't even register I was there. She was mumbling to herself. I remember being surprised at how fast she moved—"

"Wait, what?" This gets my attention almost as much as listening to him tell his story. My mind careens back to my dream. "You saw her running through the woods?"

"Yeah. I have no idea why, but the sight of her, well…It kinda freaked me out. It was the only reason I was able to get up and leave, otherwise I'd probably still be sitting there…" He gives me a small smile, which I return. "Why do you ask?"

"I had this dream the other night. It sounds like what you saw…" A chill runs up my spine, subsequently followed by a thought that all but makes me break into a cold sweat.

"Oh my God. You don't think my mom could have heard our conversation that day, do you?" Of course, at that point, my parents knew I was leaving, but what they didn't know was that I was leaving the next day…And, of course, that I'd been pregnant.

"I really doubt that, Em," Bryan says as he places a comforting hand on my knee. "I'd been out there for a while, way too long for your mom to have eavesdropped on us and then decided to take a stroll through the woods."

A modicum of relief washes over me, just enough to prevent my impending heart attack.

71

"Em." Bryan scoots closer to me, letting his hand slide between my legs and wrap around the back of my knee, gently massaging it. "I just need to say something." He takes a deep breath. "When you left, I actually hated you. Or, at least, I'd convinced myself that I hated you. I reasoned that hating you was a helluva lot easier than missing you." I watch his Adam's apple bob. "But really…I think I was just hating myself. I mean…I was the one who got you pregnant—"

"Bryan," I interject, but he stops me with a small squeeze to my knee.

"No, wait. Let me finish. I got us into that mess, Emma. I wasn't careful enough. I was the one who found that clinic that fucked everything up. I was the one who wanted everything to go back to the way it was, completely ignoring how much you were actually hurting…fuck…" He drops his head, letting loose a dismal laugh. "Fuck, Emma, I'm so sorry."

Seeing tears in his eyes is enough to bring tears to mine.

"Bryan…I don't think it was anyone's fault. It just…happened. And it's my damn fault I didn't handle it better. Maybe if I'd been honest about how I really felt…"

"We could do this all night, Emma. Blaming ourselves, blaming each other. But what is that really going to accomplish?"

I see his point, and yet I still feel like I need to apologize again, over and over, until the phrase "I'm sorry" becomes an antiquated banality.

"I'm still sorry," I say.

He gives me a sad smile as he says, "I'm sorry too."

We look into each others eyes and for the second time, first with Heidi and now with Bryan, I feel a thread of tranquility ease through me, loosening some of the knots that have been inside me for so long. It feels so good.

"How's all this going, by the way?" He nods his head towards the copious amounts of boxes.

"It's moving along," I sigh. "I've pretty much got everything downstairs packed up. Still need to do my parents' room and their bathroom. And I should take a look at the attic, make sure nothing's up there. The Red Cross is coming Friday to pick up the furniture for donation. So yeah...I guess it's going well." And yet, I don't feel much pride in my work.

"So...After Friday, you're leaving..." It's not so much a question as it is a statement.

"Yeah, I guess so," is my noncommittal answer.

He bobs his head in understanding. He releases my knee and stands from the couch, walking the length of the room.

"Are you keeping anything?" He asks as he pokes through a box of books.

"A few things. I'm bringing the grandfather clock with me, as well as my mom's desk and hope chest. And, you know, a few other little things."

"Damn, your mom had a lot of books," he laughs.

"No kidding. It took me forever to pack up. I am keeping what would appear to be her favorite book, *The Bell Jar.* It looks like she read it a hundred times."

"Huh...Interesting." I can practically see the inner workings of his brain firing into action.

"What is?"

"That *The Bell Jar* would be her favorite book." He registers the confusion on my face. "Have you never read it?"

"No," I laugh. "Clearly, I have not."

"It's about a woman who goes insane, Em."

A tingling starts at the base of my spine. My eyes travel around the sea of boxes as I try and rack my brain for any other book that looked as used as that one. I come up empty.

73

"That has to be a coincidence," I say lamely.

"Just like you dreaming about something that happened eight years ago?"

Point taken.

"Where's the book?" He asks as he watches me stand from my curled-up position. We both have a mind to look at this thing a little more closely.

"My bedroom." I lead the way upstairs. I'm keenly aware of Bryan's eyes on my butt, and maybe it's the wine in me, but I make a point to swagger my hips a little more than I normally would.

Bryan slows as he enters my room, taking in the empty shelves, bare walls, and unmade bed.

"I never could enter this room when I'd visit your parents," he admits, almost to himself. "It was just too painful." I can only imagine. All the times we made love in here (unbeknownst to my parents), all the nights up late talking, planning our future together...This room is a relic to a once solid relationship.

I don't trust myself to open my mouth, so instead I lift the lid of my suitcase and pull out the book. I remove the bubble wrap and hand it over to Bryan, who examines the spine with interest. He flips through the book, but if he finds anything, he doesn't say.

"I dunno, Em. It just seems weird." His eyes travel to the box of memorabilia I'm reclaiming from my room. "Is this all the stuff you're keeping?" As I nod he places *The Bell Jar* on the bed and kneels down to examine the contents, pulling out my high school yearbook. He opens the front cover and starts reading what all my friends had written me, a small smile playing on his lips. I'm so enraptured by this smile that I don't even notice his picture and the poem "Anywhere With You" falling from within the pages, fluttering to land facedown at his feet.

I dive for it the same instant he stoops to pick it up.

"What's thi—" His voice cuts off as he stares at his findings, now firmly clasped between my fingers and his. I try like hell to keep the blush down but I may as well dunk my head in red paint for all the good it's doing.

"You were going to keep these?" He asks gently. I nod mutely. "Why?"

Try being transparent just once in your life, Emma.

I look up into his eyes and say, "Because I couldn't let you go."

It's ironic, really. Here I've been trying to escape this place and the second I'm back in the depths of the redwoods, it's like I've never left.

I take the yearbook from Bryan's hands and place it on my desk along with his picture and poem. I move into his personal space. I place my hands on his taut abdomen and slowly start to run them up the length of his torso, feeling every ridge I once had memorized. I feel his breathing pick up as he looks down at me with a fever in his eyes that I know all too well. His hands slide up my arms and come to cup my face. As he leans down to kiss me, I can't help but feel like I'm sealing my fate.

~~~

I'm hiking in the forest behind my house. The sun's streaming through the trees, casting abstract shadows across my bare arms. I keep my eyes trained on the ground, feeling like I'm looking for something, but I'm not entirely sure what that something is.

"Emma! Emma, wait up!" Bryan's running up to me, holding a bundle in his arms. He smiles at me as he slows and finally stops. "You almost forgot this." He hands it to me and steps back, like he's expecting me to unwrap it. I see that it's a dishtowel and whatever's inside it is cold to the touch. The dishtowel itself is embroidered with little red poppy flowers.

"You are so beautiful," Bryan says as he reaches out a hand to caress my cheek. I smile until I notice his hand is covered in blood.

"Oh my God, Bryan! Your hand! Are you okay?!" I set the bundle down and reach out to examine him, only to find that mine, too, is covered in blood. I glance down at the bundle, only then realizing that it's not little red poppies decorating the towel, but splotches of crimson blood.

Both Bryan and I gasp and fall back onto our bottoms as the towel unwraps itself. We watch in rapt horror as Mom unfurls from its bloody material. She's crying like a newborn baby, sputtering about how the devil corrupted Dad.

"It's all his fault! It's all his fault!" She screams.

~~~

Muted sunlight filters through my window. I crack open my eyes and see the redwoods are veiled with a thick coat of fog so dense that I can barely see past the tree line. *Go figure.*

I roll onto my back and stretch, only slightly surprised when I feel a firm arm snake around my stomach and pull me up against an even firmer chest.

Bryan breathes in my scent, rubbing his nose against the back of my neck. How that can make me tingly is anyone's guess.

"Good morning, beautiful." His voice is raspy from nonuse. "How did you sleep?"

Considering the warped dream I've just woken from, one would think I'd feel like a bag of rocks. But I don't. I feel surprisingly alert. And satisfied. And sore. Hell, I'm damn near jovial.

I roll over so I'm face-to-face with an adorably rumpled Bryan.

"I slept well, aside for the totally twisted dream I just had," I say as I fold my hands under my head and snuggle a little closer to his warmth.

"Tell me about it." He tucks a strand of hair behind my ear, an amorous gesture I'd forgotten about. I describe my dream to him in full detail. Clearly the two dreams I've had are related, but their message isn't quite so obvious. And frankly, I don't want to spend my last few days here worrying about it.

"You have a very active imagination, Emma," Bryan laughs.

I smile as I strain my arm across his broad chest to check the time on my phone. It's seven in the morning. I have a few hours before Heidi gets here. Time to put my dream behind me.

I straddle Bryan's lap, laughing at his startled face and then going serious as I lean down to give him the first of many kisses. When he enters me the dream is all but dust in the wind.

Chapter 7

Bryan went home to shower and change his clothes, saying he'd return short-ly to help me and Heidi with my parents' room. I'm floating on a cloud of postcoital euphoria as I move about the house, first to shower away the evidence of our lovemaking, then to the kitchen to start a pot of coffee.

I realize I'm playing with fire by sleeping with Bryan, but the fact of the matter is that I can't bring myself to care. Sure, I'd had a few lovers in New York, but there was always something absent, a deficiency that I couldn't pinpoint. I realize now it was the emotional component that comes when being intimate with someone. I didn't care about those men. How could I when I've been in love with the same man for over a freaking decade?

And there's no denying that fact, not after last night. I'm in love with Bryan. I tried to run from it. I tried to hide from it. But it's so explicitly clear that I'd have to be a real moron to not, at the very least, acknowledge the fact or, better yet, find a way to make it work.

"Maybe Bryan would move to New York," I say to the house. It responds by creaking solemnly, as if telling me it, also, doesn't want me to leave.

"I mean, it's not totally out of the realm of possibility," I reason. "His trade is marketable anywhere, in high demand and, plus, he'd probably make more money in New York than here anyways."

But what about Eureka? My mind whispers at me.

"What about Eureka? I don't even like it here." I say the words out loud, but inside I know that's not true. Since I've made amends with Heidi, I've felt that Eureka has regained some of its old charm. And now, with Bryan…Let's just say that the fog crowding the forest outside my windows doesn't seem so depressing. The gravitas of the redwoods trees, which just a few days ago felt oppressive, suddenly doesn't feel so suffocating.

If you stay here, you'll end up like Mom…

"That's ridiculous! I'm not crazy…"

78

"Dude…Are you talking to yourself?" Heidi's voice startles me so much the mug I'm holding slips from my hands and shatters at my feet.

"Shit," I hiss. I kneel to the floor and start collecting shards of mug.

"Sorry to frighten you," she says sheepishly. "The door was open, so I just let myself in." She drops her purse on the counter and stoops to help me clean up.

"It's okay. I was just…Well yeah, I was talking to myself." I laugh.

She gives me a coy smile. "So…What happened last night?"

I bite back a grin as I say, rather primly, "A lady never tells."

Her eyes get as round as saucers and she breaks into a huge grin.

"You hooked up!" She practically shrieks with glee. "You hooked up! You hooked up!" Despite holding a handful of sharp slivers, Heidi stands and starts doing a happy dance around the kitchen, making me laugh so hard I feel a stitch form in my side. "I knew it! I freaking knew it! Oh my God, you have to tell me everything!"

"I'm not giving you a blow-by-blow," I laugh as we dump the mug into the trash.

"I'm sure you gave Bryan a blow-by-blow!"

"Good grief, Heidi!" I laugh.

"Oh, come on! Don't be so square!" *Hadn't I just asked myself that the other day?* "Is he still just as good as before?" She wiggles her eyebrows at me. Oh, how teenage girls share everything…

I chuckle and make the decision to not be square.

"He's better," I say. "He's the best sex I've had in eight years, if I'm being honest with you."

"While I hate the idea of another man touching you, I'm pleased to know I haven't lost my touch." Bryan's all cocky grins as he enters the kitchen, carrying a to-go bag of donuts that smells amazing.

"Doesn't anyone knock anymore?" I mock-complain.

He walks right up to me and gives me a long, lingering kiss, a promise of what's to come later this evening. My toes actually curl.

"Jesus, get a room," I hear Heidi mumble. Our laugher breaks the canoodling.

We grab some coffee and go about distributing donuts. Bryan even remembered to get an apple fritter, my favorite. The easy repartee between us is just like back in high school. It's as though I never left, really. The hollowness I've felt for so long is leisurely starting fill up and it both excites and scares me. It excites me because I finally don't feel dead inside. But it scares me because the one thing I promised myself, to never come back to Eureka, is patently at risk.

~~~

My parents' room is large and filled to the gills. On top of Mom sliding into dementia, it would appear she was also toying with the boundaries of hoarding.

"This makes the downstairs look like a walk in the park," I huff as we stand shoulder to shoulder, like soldiers standing at the front line in battle. My gaze rolls over the piles of clothes, books, boxes, papers...My God, it's like looking at a landfill. Not to mention all her little trinkets garnishing every available surface area.

"We just put our noses to the ground and get it done. I don't know why, but it creeps me out to be in here." Heidi actually shudders. I can't say I blame her. I myself have a weird tingling sensation running up and down my spine, as if Mom's ghost is standing behind me and breathing down my neck...

"Right. Okay." I shake myself and dump my armload of boxes on the floor. "Heidi, how about you start putting the boxes together with Bryan and I'll start sorting through all this stuff."

"On it."

I ease forward, trying to decide where to start first. As if sensing my mounting anxiety, Bryan lays a hand on my shoulder and gives it a small squeeze.

"Don't get overwhelmed, Em." He places a kiss at my temple, idly tucking a strand of hair behind my ear. I give him a grateful smile and decide to tackle the clothes first. It seems logical since there are piles upon piles scattered all over the room.

"I had no idea my mom was such a fashionista," I say as I start dismembering a particularly large pile of clothes, creating separate stacks for her shirts, pants, and dresses. The labels reveal designer duds, clothing I certainly can't afford. Mom was always a petit lady and since I inherited her slender frame, I have no doubt I could reuse some of these clothes. Except...Do I really want to wear the clothes of a woman who went crazy?

As if answering me, the house lets off a groan that actually gives us all pause, like we're worried the foundation may crack and the house will come crashing down on us.

"Is it just me or does it suddenly feel like this place is haunted?" Heidi asks, her eyes roaming around the ceiling, searching for ghosts, no doubt.

"The house? No. This room? Abso-fucking-lutely." Bryan says.

"I suppose it would, since this is where Mom spent most of her time the last two years. Clearly," I add with a wide sweep of my hand.

"I'm really glad you're not doing this alone, Emma. I'd be freaking out." As if to prove her point, Heidi starts assembling boxes faster.

I can't imagine doing this alone either, now that Heidi and Bryan are back in my life. Being in this room by myself would careen me into yet another panic attack.

No wonder I saved this room for last...

We work in silence for a while, the only sounds coming from the rustle of cardboard and clothing. Once every box is put together, they join me in organizing Mom's clothes. I leave the piles to them while I tackle her closet. Before long, we have a nice rhythm going and the room starts to clear up as more and more of her possessions get packed away.

"Okay, it's waaaaay too quiet in here," Heidi exclaims randomly. "Is there a radio in here or something?"

"I think so…" I wade over to the bedside table and lift a pile of papers to reveal the alarm clock…And an untouched copy of *The Bell Jar*. I pick it up, letting the smooth surface glide through my hands. I fan through it, the smell of new book wafting into my face.

"Is that another copy of *The Bell Jar*?" Bryan asks.

"Yes…But it looks completely untouched."

"Lemme see." He raises his hands, so I toss him the book and take my stack of papers to one of the many trash bags we have positioned in the hall. I do a quick scan to make sure nothing important is hidden within the pages, but it looks like a bunch of random flyers and junk mail. *Why did you keep this, Mom?*

"Yeah, this copy is brand-spanking new," Bryan confirms as I enter the room.

"Someone wanna tell me what's going on?" Heidi asks.

I take the book from Bryan and place it in the small pile of stuff I'm keeping. "When I was cleaning out the library downstairs, I came across a copy of that book that looked like it was read about eight thousand times. It just seems weird that Mom would have another copy of the same book."

"A book about a woman who goes nuts, no less," Bryan adds.

"Well that's…creepy," Heidi says. I watch her green eyes scan the ceiling yet again.

"No kidding," I mumble as I resume my tackling of her closet. All the clothes are out, so I kneel to the floor and start pulling out boxes of shoes and other paraphernalia I'm sure Mom never touched. "Oh! Music!" I jump to my feet and turn on the little radio. The oldies station starts up, The Mamas and The Papas singing about Monday, Monday. "Much better."

We work all the way up until lunch. The only reason we stop is because I can hear their stomachs grumbling with hunger.

Before we head downstairs, we survey the work we've done. The room is still cluttered with Mom's trinkets and other random nonsense, but for the most part it's cleaned up and boxed away.

"Let's take the full boxes downstairs, make some more room up here, and then I'll run to town for some lunch," Bryan suggests.

"Sounds great," Heidi and I say in unison.

We haul box after box downstairs and place them with all the others in the living room.

When Bryan leaves, Heidi and I head back upstairs to start on Mom's trinkets. I realize I also have to go through her desk and the hope chest, just to make sure nothing valuable lies within them.

"I'm gonna start in on Mom's desk," I say.

"I'll get on all these knickknacks," Heidi says, pulling out a swathe of bubble wrap. "Do you wanna keep any of these?" I scan the expanse of baubles, registering that many of these figurines I don't remember from my childhood. *How much money was Mom spending?!*

"Naw, it's okay. I'm sure the Red Cross would appreciate them."

I roll the top of Mom's desk up, mildly shocked that everything within the little cubbies is perfectly organized. Compared to the room, this is a welcome surprise.

I start pulling out neat stacks of paper, leafing through bills that have been paid based off the dates penned across the top of each page in my mother's signature, loopy handwriting. Apparently she was still lucid enough to pay the electric bill on time.

As I sift through her desk, I can't help but notice that Mom really was two different people. On the one hand, she was a devoted mother, wife, and nurse. And friend, apparently, based off all the condolence cards I've received over the past week. But then she flipped, did a complete180 into this deranged woman who terrorized Daisy and holed away in this house until death finally took her in her sleep. *What could have possibly happened to her to make that switch?* Yes, I realize crazy runs in this family, but it seemed like it was just overnight that she turned. I've always used the market crash as my signifier for when things went sideways...But maybe that's just a coincidence. After all, it wasn't much longer after that when I had the abortion in my junior year.

The Mystics start singing about love, pulling me back from my musings about Mom and turning my mind towards Bryan...A welcome distraction.

I continue to toss out papers, not coming across anything of interest until I uncover a stack of letters neatly tied together with twine. I pull them out, noticing that they are addressed to my father but have no returning address on them. Odd. I stick them in my meager "keep" pile to examine later.

"Man alive, your mom had a ton of stuff!" Heidi randomly exclaims. I can't help but laugh.

"Yes, she did. I guess hoarding was part of the decline."

"I'm back!" We hear Bryan holler from downstairs. Since Mom's bedroom is on the back side of the house, we didn't hear his truck pull up. I'm surprised to see that it's been almost forty minutes since Bryan left. *How long have I been sitting here thinking about Mom?*

"Thank God! I'm so freaking hungry," Heidi laughs.

We abandon our work and go downstairs. Bryan is laying out our sandwiches around the dining room table, complete with bags of chips and sodas. I can't help but notice his eyes going soft when he sees me, a little fact that makes my heart flutter.

"How's it going up there?" He asks as he wraps an arm around my waist, placing a soft kiss on my neck.

"It's coming along, actually. Her trinkets are almost packed away. I just have to finish her desk and the hope chest." I try to control my hormones as his tongue draws a provocative line along my collar bone.

"Jesus, Bryan, control yourself," Heidi laughingly admonishes.

"It's been eight years, Heidi. Leave me alone."

We're laughing as we take our seats and start digging into lunch. Now that I'm outside the confines of Mom's cave, I'm feeling lighter and happier. There's something about that room that weighs me down, like her ghost is sitting there, watching us, chiding me for not being here when she needed me most. Although… I can't say I'd blame her for that. Even still, I'll be happy to have that room cleared out.

We don't speak much, but that's only because we have our mouths full of food. The ache in my stomach slowly subsides as I wolf down my sandwich, delighting in the fact that Bryan's hand stays on my leg the whole time we eat. He absently strokes it, like he's not even realizing he's doing it. It does, however, turn my mind to a very dirty place and I once again have to control my hormones.

By the time we finish eating, I'm practically panting like a dog.

Tone it down, Emma. I'd hoped last night would curb my appetite for sex, but I guess it just fueled the fire.

We throw away our trash and trek back upstairs, my mind still in the gutter. Thank God I had an IUD put in place a few years back, because if last night and this morning are any indication, Bryan and I will be having sex multiple times over the next few days. Given my past, I never really thought my libido would come back. Clearly I was just waiting for Bryan.

The lightness I felt just a few minutes ago dissolves (along with my hormones) the moment I walk into Mom's room.

"Fuck, this place is oppressive," Heidi exclaims. I'm glad I'm not the only one who feels it.

"Okay…Let's just get this over with," I say distractedly, eyeing the desk and wondering if I can't just dump all the contents into the trash.

"How about I start on the bathroom, Em?" Bryan offers. "I sincerely doubt there's anything in there you're gonna wanna keep." I give him yet another grateful smile as he squeezes my hand and goes into the adjoining ensuite, grabbing a trash bag along the way.

I resume my spot at the desk and continue to empty out all the little cubbies. Letters aside, I don't come across anything else of interest. I heave a sigh of relief when I roll the top down and give it a gentle pat. I've always loved this piece of furniture…

"See all the little compartments?" Mom asks me. I'm seven years old, sitting on her lap as she shows me all the hidden cubbies inside her desk. "This is where people used to hide their secrets. If you didn't want anyone to find something, you could always just hide it away in one of these column drawers." She demonstrates by pulling on a tall, slender drawer disguised as a baluster. "Pretty cool, huh?"

86

It was that very pillar where I found those letters addressed to my dad. I really want to read them, but I don't want to give up precious time before the Red Cross comes tomorrow.

"What are those?" Heidi asks as she looks down at them resting in my hands.

"Letters to my dad...I'm not sure who they're from."

"Mysterious," Heidi jokes. *Mysterious indeed.* "I'm all done with the trinkets, babe. Want help with your mom's chest?"

"That would be great, thank you." I set the letters on top of *The Bell Jar,* pledging to myself to read them later tonight. Maybe tucked under a blanket with Bryan by my side...

I give myself a little shake, not even bothering to hold down the blush as inappropriate imagines flood my brain. We kneel down in front of the hope chest and raise the lid, the scent of redwood and time wafting into our faces. *How long has it been since this has been opened?*

I'm looking down into what can only be catalogued as organized chaos. The hope chest was meant to hold all my mom's arts and crafts, everything from scrapbooking to needlework to knitting. Crafting was a love of hers only slightly overshadowed by books.

The chest served its purpose well, in light of all the crap shoved into these four walls. We start pulling out balls of yarn, magazines, endless tubes of glue... *My God, it's amazing what Mom kept a hold of!*

The Guess Who starts singing about having no time, making me smile because this was one of my favorite songs growing up. Dad always did a great impression of this song. He loved harmonizing, a memory that makes my smile broaden. He was always trying to get me to sing along with him, but I was too shy, afraid my voice would crack or I'd be horribly off-key.

There's nothing I wish to keep until we get to the very bottom of the chest, where we come upon a scrapbook with a picture of me, Mom, and Dad glued to the front. It's a picture I remember all too well. It was taken the day I left for college. I reach for it like I might reach for a live bomb. It's a huge book, its cover damn-near bursting at the seams for all the memorabilia inside. My fingers itch to open the cover, but I know that if I do that I won't be able to put it down, and I still have way too much packing to do.

"This looks interesting," Bryan says from behind us. He kneels down and runs a hand over the picture. "Who took this?"

"It was on a timer," I say, swallowing down a lump in my throat. "Mom insisted on a picture. I'm not sure why…No one looks particularly happy." And that's the understatement of the century. My eighteen-year-old self is standing between Mom and Dad, a tight smile smeared across her face like an especially bitter jam. This younger version of me stands rigid as a statue, boney shoulders up at her ears like she's waiting for someone to smack her. Mom's face is red and splotchy because she'd only stopped crying long enough to insist upon a picture. Dad's bloodshot eyes stare at the camera like he's not even seeing it. His usually smiling face isn't smiling here…It's as grave as a freaking tombstone.

"Why the hell did Mom use this picture as a cover for her scrapbook?" I ask.

I'm answered with silence. Clearly, no one can understand the inner workings of a crazy lady's mind. I set the scrapbook aside, along with the letters, and we finish pulling out all of Mom's stuff from the chest. Bryan, who's finished with the bathroom, boxes items that can be reused and throws out the rest. I can't help but notice it odd that for all the art and craft supplies Mom had, she has very little to show for it, the one scrapbook aside. I've come across none of the blankets, scarves, or knitted caps I remember from my childhood. It really depresses me.

"What happened to it all?" I ask to no one in particular.

"Maybe she gave it all away," Bryan suggests.

"Yeah...Yeah, I suppose."

Much like when we entered this room this morning, we all stand shoulder to shoulder and survey the work done. The room is now completely devoid of any traces of Mom. It's abnormally unsettling, like I'm erasing her from existence.

"So that's it then, right?" Heidi asks, "I mean...All the rooms are packed up?"

"Looks that way." I don't know why this makes me so sad. Wasn't it just a few days ago that I was looking forward to this moment? Because it meant I could pack up the U-Haul and get out of dodge? But I feel Bryan's and Heidi's shoulders press into mine and I feel no such satisfaction.

"Lets move the rest of these boxes downstairs, Em. Make it easier on the workers tomorrow," Bryan says, going to the alarm clock and switching it off. Bob Dylan's voice is abruptly cut off. He unplugs it and places it in the last box we've yet to tape up.

"Yeah...Yeah, okay." I place the scrapbook and letters on one of the boxes and ferry it downstairs. It takes us several trips, but eventually her room is clear, sans the heavy furniture. We toss the garbage bags out by the trash and arrange the boxes according to room. I don't know if that will make it easier on the workers, but it can't hurt. Plus, it keeps me busy while I try and tamp down these feelings of nostalgia.

I glance at my phone and see that it's almost three o'clock. I'm surprised by how long that actually took considering I had two other people helping me. Gratitude blossoms in my chest. If not for them, I don't think I could have gotten everything ready for tomorrow. Which reminds me...

"Oh crap! I still need to check out the attic!" And here I thought I was done. I glance longingly at the letters and scrapbook. *Good things come to those who wait, Emma.*

"If you two wanna take off, go for it," I say. "You've already done so much for me." Why I want to cry right now is beyond me. Maybe because that gratitude is filling up my chest and pushing other emotions to the surface.

Bryan comes up behind me and enfolds me against his chest.

"I'm not going anywhere," he whispers into my ear, giving my neck another soft stroke of his lips. I involuntary shiver because it feels that damned good. I can tell he's smiling into my hair, no doubt proud of the effect he has on me.

"No way, babe," Heidi calls from the kitchen. She comes back into the living room carrying three glasses of water. She hands me one, offers one to Bryan, and takes a huge gulp from her own. "I'm staying until the bitter end. Well, that is until you two have sex again. I don't need to catch that show."

We're all laughing as we head back upstairs.

Chapter 8

The trap door to the attic sits in the ceiling at the end of the hallway. When I pull the chain, the door drops down and I have to finagle the creaky wooden steps to the ground, not relishing the idea of heading into a vat of cobwebs. Who even knows the last time someone was up there. Dust particles dance in my face, that musty smell particular to attics attacking my sinuses. I bite back a sneeze as I ascend into the gloom.

"Wait, Em," Heidi says. She rushes into my bedroom and comes out a moment later with my little pink flashlight. "You may want this."

"How did you know I carry a flashlight in my purse?" I laugh.

"Because it's you, Emma. Always the prepared one." She gives me a knowing wink. I can't begrudge her that.

I click on the light and grip it between my lips as I grasp the railings, hauling myself up the short ladder into what feels like another world.

Another world within another world…

The attic is huge, spanning the entire length of the house. The one circular window that sits at the other end of the room is just about worthless. Years of dust have completely obscured it, casting what little light there is up here into dreary shadows. I scan for spiderwebs before I heft myself all the up, my neurosis for insects keeping me on high alert.

I squint into the drab light, making my way towards the center of the room where the ceiling is the highest. I scan the rafters for any eight-legged friends. The last thing I need is one dropping on my head. The asinine thought actually makes my stomach clench.

I pass the flashlight over my head, satisfied that nothing's going to attack me. Only then do I focus on the attic itself, the long, narrow space reminding me of an oversized coffin.

And from the looks of it, totally empty. I'm almost convinced there's nothing up here when my light falls on a box that's tucked into the back of the room, practically hidden from view.

As if they can sense it, Bryan pokes his head up. "See anything?"

"Yeah…" I say as I tentatively make my way towards the box, stooping low so as not to smack my head. As I get closer, I cast my light over it. It's nondescript, a simple cardboard box, but when I go to move it towards the trapdoor I find that it's ridiculously heavy. *I'm gonna have to use some muscle on this one.* I tug it out of the corner and shift around so I can start pushing it towards Bryan, keeping a keen eye for any critters.

"This is really heavy, Bryan," I warn as I nudge it closer to the opening, slightly embarrassed at how out of breath I am. "Just be careful when lifting it down."

It takes me, Bryan and Heidi's brawn to get the dusty thing down to the second floor. I'm all too happy to close up the attic…Even as a child, I didn't like it up there.

"Should we take it downstairs?" Heidi asks, wiping dust from her hands onto her jeans. I myself could use a shower. I feel like I've got bugs crawling up and down my neck.

"Lets see what's inside first," I suggest. "It's really damn heavy."

"My money's on books," Bryan says.

"A likely possibility," I laugh. I kneel down and start to pull the tape off the top, that scratchy sound making the hair on my arms stand up. I flip the tabs up, not even registering what I'm seeing until it's scuttling out of the box towards me. I screech unabashedly and scurry back on my hands as the biggest (and fastest!) spider I've ever seen in my entire life makes his grand entrance. You may as well stick me in the deepest recesses of hell. I watch it plop to the floor and scuttle towards me. I swear it can smell my fear.

I think I may throw up when Bryan's boot comes down on top of it—*is that a crunch I heard?!*—effectively ending its life. I look up to see Bryan's amused face smiling down at me, Heidi guffawing behind him.

"It's not funny!" I practically cry.

"Oh my God, you are such a wuss when it comes to spiders," Heidi titters.

"Are you freaking kidding me? That wasn't a spider. That was a goddamned alien!"

"Heidi, would you grab me some toilet paper? Emma doesn't need to see this." He speaks to her but his eyes never leave me. My face goes warm under his stare. It's like the hero undressing the damsel in distress with his eyes after saving her from the dragon. Granted, it *was* just a spider, but still…

I get to my feet and ease my body against his.

"Thank you," I whisper against his lips, sighing happily when I feel his breath catch.

"Here." Heidi's still laughing as she hands a wad of toilet paper to Bryan. "You clean that up while Emma and I see what's in the box…Maybe more spiders?!" Her mock-horror reminds me of Munch's painting *The Scream*. I can't help but laugh. My aversion towards spiders is, for all intents and purposes, kinda embarrassing.

"I'm glad my psychoneurosis amuses you, babe." I give Bryan one more squeeze as I ease around him, averting my eyes from the mess on the floor. I approach the box with care. I know I'm being a baby, but I truly can't take spiders. The aversion started when I was about eleven years old. I'd put on my nightgown, getting ready for bed. I looked onto my shoulder and found a huge, fat spider just sitting there, staring at me. When I screamed, I'd scared it enough to bite me, giving me a welt the size of a coaster on my shoulder that hurt and itched like hell. It was enough to nearly give me a heart attack and officially make me an arachnophobic.

Heidi eases the flaps open and we stare down at a view that makes my blood stop in my veins. I almost, *almost*, wish I were staring at more spiders.

93

"What the fuck?" Heidi leans over, pulling out a copy of *The Bell Jar*, the first of many, it would appear. "She has a whole box of these?" Heidi's confused face is just the tip of the iceberg for me. I'm loath to touch anything that had a spider on it, but I can't help myself and reach in to pull a copy out myself. Bryan comes to my side and lets off a soft whistle.

"That. Is. Weird," is all he says. It's the exact same copy of the one I found in her room, yet different from the one in her library. These have just the title printed across a black cover in a flowing magenta script. The one I kept for myself has a blurry picture of a woman on the cover, an eery image for any book, let alone one about a woman gone crazy.

I flip to the first few pages, taking note of the year this edition was published.

"Published in 2006," I say to no one in particular.

"Yeah...so?"

I'm so lost in thought that I don't even know who asks this. I drop the book in the box and head to my room, grabbing the worn copy from my suitcase and seeing that this edition was published in 2000.

"What are you thinking Emma?" Bryan asks as he wraps a sturdy arm around my body, a body that feels like it's about to get carried away on even the slightest puff of wind.

"Those were all published six years after this one," I look down at the hazy image of the woman and shudder. "And it was around that time that I got pregnant..."

"Check this out," Heidi says as she enters my room. "It's a packing slip. These were published in 2006, but your mom didn't actually buy up that case until 2008-"

"My junior year..." Dread sets in my stomach like an ugly boil.

94

We all look at each other, thinking the exact same thing but not having the nerve to speak it out loud. *It can't be a coincidence that Mom ordered a case of this book the same year I had my freaking abortion...She had to have known.*

"Let's bring the books downstairs and figure out what the hell is going on, okay?" Bryan lays a heartened hand on my shoulder and gives it a small rub. I clutch my copy of *The Bell Jar* to my chest, nodding mutely. An ice is running through my veins that I've only ever felt two other times in my life; the first was when I told Heidi I was leaving, the second, when I told Bryan.

He carries the box downstairs with me and Heidi in tow. Even in shocked horror, I can still appreciate the way his arms strain against the fabric of his shirt, that tattoo, which happens to be a Celtic band honoring his heritage, rippling under the weight of the books. He places the box on the living room floor and joins us in the dining room. I ease into a chair, suddenly feeling very old. I place Mom's book on the table and stare at it.

Obviously she read this book several times before she went ahead and purchased a case-full. Why would she do that? I flip the book open to the first page, noticing a line highlighted in faded yellow: "'I thought it must be the worst thing in the world.'" Both Heidi and Bryan look at me from across the table.

"I feel tired," I sigh. I finger the edge of the book, wishing that the answers would just fall from the sky so I wouldn't have to sit here and ponder what happened to Mom all those years ago.

"Why don't you go lie down, Em?" Heidi suggests. "There's really nothing else to do until the Red Cross comes tomorrow." She glances down at her watch. "And besides, I should probably swing by the office...My crew is good, but they're not as good as me," she adds with a wink.

"Will I see you tomorrow?" A panicky feeling flutters in my chest at the thought of not seeing her again.

"Of course! Like I said...The bitter end." She walks around the table and wraps an arm around my shoulders, giving the top of my head a kiss. "If you need anything, don't hesitate to call me, okay? Although," I can tell she's eyeing Bryan, a smile in her voice. "You probably won't need to." She gives me one more squeeze, claps Bryan on the shoulder and then she's out the door.

Bryan comes to sit in the chair next to me, running a hand down my arm.

"Em, I can see the wheels turning in your head." This makes me laugh because he's absolutely right. "Let's turn it off for the night, okay? We can address all this shit tomorrow."

It's an immediate reaction but suddenly I'm out of my chair and straddling his lap. I wrap my arms around his neck and meet his lips with a lust so strong it almost takes my breath away. I feel his fingers dig into my hips, run up my spine, curve around my butt. It's like he can't decide where to touch first. It doesn't matter, though, because just as quickly as I was in his lap, I'm out of it. Our lips don't separate as my hands deftly unbutton my jeans and his. I'm not sure where this urgency has come from, but I know I need every ounce of Bryan I can possibly get.

Chapter 9

When we finally come up for air, it's after six. I've never made love that long in my entire life. The whole downstairs has been christened. As I watch Bryan roll onto his back on the living room floor, I can't help but think it was a way to inculcate some merriment in rooms I've come to associate with sadness.

"Jesus, Emma." Bryan languidly stretches. "Where did that come from?" His eyes are glazed over, a lazy smile spreading across his face. He's never looked more handsome.

"I could ask you the same thing," I laugh.

96

"That came from eight years of keeping you in my spank bank, that's where."

I laugh as I roll to my side and prop my head up on my hand. I run my other hand across his flexed stomach, marveling at the sheer beauty one person can possess.

"Well, that time for me was fairly dry as well."

"Only fairly?" He cocks an eyebrow at me.

"Yes...fairly." I have the good grace to blush.

"What's your magic number, Em?" I knew this question was coming and yet I still inwardly flinch.

"What's yours?"

"Why are you deflecting?"

I laugh. "Because I can."

"Not with me."

And isn't that the truth. Bryan can read me like a book. Even when we first got together, I could never lie to him because he'd always call me on it.

"It's not that many," I humor. "Including you..." I pause, thinking. "Only seven." I see his jaw twitch a few times before relaxing. I don't doubt he hates thinking of me with other men, mainly because he said it just this morning. "What about you?" I ask playfully, trying to bring that smile back to his face. I drape a leg over his, just now realizing that we are conversing in the living room of my childhood home stark naked. How times have changed.

He smiles as he says, "It's unquestionably more than seven."

"Is that so?" I can tell he's trying to make me jealous, but I refuse to take the bait.

"Oh yeah," he laughs. "I had to sleep with a lot of women to get you out of my head. And look where it got me." As he says this he pulls me on top of him, eliciting from me a small squeal. He brushes the hair from my face and pulls my mouth to his, his tongue tracing my bottom lip. "No matter what, though, it was always you I dreamt about. It was always you I wanted." He becomes serious. "And now that I have you back, Death himself is my only contender."

I don't have time to consider his words before he's inside me again.

~~~

After we shower, we head down to the kitchen to find something to eat. I didn't realize how hungry I was until after we stopped having sex. Who knew lovemaking could build up such an appetite?

"Do you want something to drink?" I ask, pulling a bottle of white wine from the fridge.

"Absolutely." He pulls down the two wine glasses I kept. "What do you have to eat around here?" I hand him the bottle to open as I scour the fridge. My food supply hasn't dwindled much. I pull out the rotisserie chicken, some salad, and decide on some rice pilaf.

I set the temperature on the oven to heat up the chicken and go about preparing the rice. Bryan hands me a hearty glass of wine, clinking his glass against mine as he leans in to give me a soft kiss. It could easily turn into something more, so I'm the one to pull away first, letting my hunger trump my hormones.

"Want some music?" He asks.

"Sure, that would be great."

He turns on the stereo and Simon and Garfunkel start harmonizing about a boxer. While this has always been a favorite song of mine, I can't help but feel melancholy when I hear it. I guess because the message seems so dismal, or at least what I perceive the message to be. I can see Dad singing along to it as he worked on his war planes, not even realizing how well his voice blended with theirs. Before I know it, I'm swallowing down a lump in my throat.

"Want me to make us a salad, Em?" Bryan's voice pulls me from my thoughts.

"Yes, thank you," I croak out.

"Hey, what's the matter?" He comes up behind me at the stove and wraps his arms around my waist.

"Ugh," I huff. "Just thinking about my dad." I measure out the amount of water for the pilaf. "He loved this song." Bryan gives my shoulder a light kiss, almost like an invitation to continue. "Did you know they both specified in their wills that they didn't want funerals? That's why I didn't have to come here. Although, I have to wonder if Mom would have had one for Dad even if he had wanted one. They seemed so estranged by the time I left, I can only imagine it got worse after that."

"The few times I came to visit, they were never in the same room together." Bryan's voice is doleful, like it's his parents he's talking about and not mine. "I'd always have to visit with them separately."

We silently watch the water start to boil, him with his arms still around me and me pressing my back into his chest, seeking comfort and support. I feel my breathing fall in rhythm with his, connecting us in one more way. Simon and Garfunkel has morphed into The Beatles, the tune much more lively. When the water's a strong simmer, I add the rice and the packaged seasoning, turn down the heat to low, and set the timer. I don't want to leave the encasement of Bryan's arms, but I disengage to put the chicken in the oven.

Bryan picks up his wine glass and takes a sip, surveying the kitchen and dining room.

"It's going to be strange seeing this place empty tomorrow," he says, almost to himself. I know what he means, though. I kind of feel like Judas, getting rid of all my parents stuff. Which reminds me…

"I really want to take a look at that scrapbook. Maybe we can do that after dinner? And those letters."

"Absolutely, Em. Whatever you need."

I prop myself up on the counter and sip my wine.

"So tell me, do you like working here?"

He shrugs. "It's alright. I'm freelance, so I can pretty much set up my own schedule, which is always nice." I nod. "What are you going to do with the house, Em?"

I can tell both our minds are orbiting around the same question: How do we stay together? Do I leave New York to live back home in Eureka? Or does Bryan take his freelance skills to The Big Apple with me?

I shrug, my gaze drawn to the forest outside the window. "I'm honestly not sure. If you'd asked me that question four days ago, I would have said sell it and never look back. But now…" My eyes find his and it's all I can do not to throw myself into his arms. "Damn, Bryan. I just don't know. I mean, I love New York. I love my job in New York. But," I pause. "I come back here and this works, too. For so long, I convinced myself that I'd outgrown Eureka, that it's just some hole-in-the-wall town I'd never come back to. It's not, though." My gaze finds the redwoods again. "It's actually spectacular…In it's own way," I add with a laugh.

Bryan comes to stand between my legs, running his free hand up my thigh.

"I love it here, Em. Everything I know is here. My friends, my family, my work." He pauses, sips his wine. "When you left, I left, too. I couldn't stand it here without you. So I went to the community college in Shasta and transferred to Berkeley after that. Even still…Humboldt managed to pull me back…And now you're here. It feels…I dunno…complete." He tucks a lock of my hair behind my ear, his hand lingering at my cheek. "And I'm selfish enough to ask you to stay." He smiles as he says this, but the weight of his words crushes down on my heart.

Wasn't I asking for this though? Didn't I think to myself the first time we made love that I was sealing my fate? And didn't he say that death itself would be the only way to lose me? My heart squeezes tighter and I close my eyes to forestall an incursion of tears. I rest my forehead against his, breathing in his scent. We relax like this for I-don't-know-how-long, long enough for the timer to go off.

"I've got it, Em," Bryan whispers. "Why don't you grab us some plates?"

I swallow and nod. I hop down from the counter and retrieve the plate from the drainer, only now realizing that I have just one plate between the two of us. *Why did I keep two wine glasses and only one plate?*

"I only have the one," I say with a small laugh, waving it in the air like a lame trophy.

"Looks like we'll be feeding each other then," Bryan says with mischief in his eyes. He pulls the chicken from the oven and starts stripping off chunks of meat. I use my one fork to spoon the pilaf onto the plate as well.

"Ah crap, I forgot the salad," Bryan says.

"Eh, who cares," I say as I toss the bag of lettuce back in the fridge. "We can make a salad later if we're still hungry."

With our lone plate—and lone fork because I'm an idiot—we head into the living room to eat. From the radio, Ten Years Later is wishing they could change the world. *I wish I could change my world…Maybe I can…*

I spy the letters and the scrapbook sitting where I'd put them this afternoon and decide I can still eat and look at pictures at the same time. I snag both items and snuggle down into the couch with Bryan.

"Shall we?" I ask.

"Yes, let's," Bryan laughs.

I set the letters aside and look at the cover of the book. I still don't understand why Mom would use such an unflattering picture as the first thing you see. Then again, Mom ranted about ghost babies and apparently had no concept of money. No joke, I'm probably donating thousands of dollars worth of clothes alone, not to mention all the porcelain and crystal doohickeys.

I open to the first page, pleasantly surprised that it's filled to the gills with pictures of me as a baby.

"Damn, I'd forgotten what a cute baby you were," Bryan laughs. His comment reminds me of the first time I brought him home to meet my parents. It was the middle of my freshman year...

"So you're Bryan," my dad says with a cool but pleasant smile.

"Yes," Bryan gulps. "It's a pleasure to meet you, sir." My fifteen-year-old self gives his hand a reassuring squeeze.

"Likewise." My mom flits up and takes Bryan by the hand, ushering him into the living room. "Please have a seat. Would you like anything? Water? Juice?"

"No, thank you, ma'am, I'm okay." I see Bryan's eyes catch a picture of me as a baby. It sits on the mantle of the fireplace. As he goes to examine it, my mom turns to me and mouths, "Soooooo good-looking!" I stifle a laugh as my dad rolls his eyes.

"Dang, Emma. You were a really cute baby."

The memory fades as quickly as it came, leaving me staring at a page dedicated to my baby cuteness and Bryan staring at me with a forkful of chicken waiting mid-air. I open my mouth so he can feed me, an oddly erotic gesture.

"Where did you go just then?" He asks.

"To the day you first met my parents," I say with a small chuckle. I run my finger over a picture of Mom holding me and smiling proudly into the camera. "She instantly liked you," I add.

"You're dad...not so much." Bryan laughs.

"Well, I think he knew on some level that you would be the one to de-flower me." I give him a playful nudge and accept an offering of rice.

"Little did he know that you were doing the same to me."

"It's different for women, though," I say absentmindedly, staring at a picture of Dad gleefully giving me a bath in the kitchen sink.

"Yeah, that's true," Bryan concedes. "I mean...It's not like we're the ones who bleed..." His voice wanes because I know he's jarred to the exact same thought his comment jarred me to: The abortion.

Drugs course through my body, numbing me from the inside out. At least, that was their goal.

The machine is loud and I can't block out the sucking sound that will no doubt permeate my dreams for years to come. It's grotesque.

The pain, even with the drugs, is unbearable.

I feel the tears fall as I watch Brian watch me. He holds my hand gently in his. His lips move but I can't hear what he's saying over the drone of the machine.

Heidi sits beside him, stroking my arm, letting her own tears stain her face.

The first shock is enough to jar my body off the table.

When another one hits I black out to the sound of both Bryan and Heidi screaming my name.

I don't say anything for several minutes. It's not that I think I'll cry if I open my mouth. It's more...What can I possibly say on the matter? I feel Bryan lean into me and kiss the side of my head, his way of acknowledging that I don't really need to say anything. He then feeds me a large bite of chicken.

"We look so normal," I say, looking back down at the photographs. "If this were the only page in this book, someone would come across it and think, 'Wow! That's a really happy family!'" I make my voice all high and chipper like they do with the bimbos in those tween movies. I'm graced with a snort from Bryan. "Little do they know what a nightmare it turned out to be." I don't even bother withholding the scorn from my voice.

"Maybe this is the whole book," Bryan says gently. "Maybe this is all your mom's most treasured memories."

"Only one way to find out," I say around a mouthful of rice.

I flip to the next page. It's still me and my parents, only I'm a little older. We still look normal. We still look happy. But of course we would. The demise of my happy family didn't happen until I was in high school.

"What do you think could be so colossal that it would drive my mom to insanity and my dad to becoming a drunk?" I don't really expect an answer. I'm more just thinking out loud. There are pictures of me in my fairy wings, laughing with Heidi. There are pictures of us out in the forest, assembling branches to make tree-houses and forts. Numerous pages show all of us on our many road trips to war memorials. Each page brings me closer and closer to adulthood. Graduating junior high and bringing me into high school is when things start to shift.

The pictures of me are still flattering, but I notice that the ones of my dad, while he's still handsome, aren't quite as complimentary. He's either blinking, looking away from the camera, or making some weird face you try to shake off before the shutter clicks. I examine each picture closely, trying to place exactly when these were taken.

Bryan has taken our plate to the kitchen and has come back with the bottle of wine to refill our glasses.

"Come across anything unusual?" He asks.

"Maybe..." I see one picture in particular where Heidi and I are wrapped up in each others arms, smiling broadly as we teeter on the precipice of a large drop-off into the ocean below. "Patrick's Point..." I mumble. The next picture shows a panoramic shot of our campsite. Dad's back is to the camera and he's got his hands on his hips, staring out at something he could only see. Because try as I may, I can't detect anything. "The one and only time we camped at Patrick's Point was at the beginning of my freshman year."

Bryan snuggles up next to me and hands me my glass. I take a sip as I flip the page...

And wine spews out of my mouth like a water fountain.

Chapter 10

"What the hell?!"

I've dumped the book on the coffee table, its cover suddenly way too hot for my hands. Both Bryan and I are standing over it, mute horror written across my face, abject confusion written across his. Never mind that I have wine all down the front of my shirt. It could be blood and I still wouldn't care.

Every single picture on the two pages we're looking at are of Dad. And every single one has his face scratched out in marks so violent, some tear through the photograph. In bright read ink written across every single picture is the word "DEVIL."

"What is this?" I whisper, kneeling down in front of the book. I can't bring myself to touch it yet, but I have to get a closer look at these photos. They look to be recent-ish...like around the beginning of my high school career. I can tell because of the clothing and Dad's haircut.

"Why would she do this?" I ask, looking up at Bryan like I expect him to have all the answers.

"Fuck, Em." Bryan runs his hands through his hair in an agitated motion. "I have no idea." He kneels down next to me. "Are the rest like this?"

I can't bring myself to touch the book, so Bryan takes charge and flips to the next page.

Affirmative. Every picture of Dad is scratched out. I'm in a few of these photos, blissfully left alone from my mothers irate scribbles. I peer more closely at the assemblage.

"That's strange," I say.

"This *is* strange, Em."

"No, I mean…All the pictures were in chronological order up until this page. Look." I point to one of me and Heidi that was taken my senior year. My face is gaunt, my collarbones protruding grotesquely from my chest. The fire and verve has completely left my face, as opposed to one directly below it taken my sophomore year. I'm walking up a trail and I must have turned around to say something to Mom because you can only see three-quarters of my face. But you can see the light in my eyes, the possibility of happiness in my smile. I'm also not an emaciated disaster. It's like comparing Pre and Post-Abortion Emma.

"Damn. You're right. It's almost like she didn't really care, just so long as she got all her pictures in." Bryan starts a soft knead along my shoulders. I hadn't even realized how tense this has made me. I take a sip of my wine, swallowing before I turn to the next page.

More pictures of my father, all scratched out. The next few pages reveal the same thing. She had apparently given up on the whole "DEVIL" branding thing. I think she made her point perfectly clear with those first two pages.

"What had my father done that would make him the devil?" I muse out loud. I flip to the next page and all but drop my glass.

"Okay, *that's* really creepy." Even Bryan's hand stills on my shoulders, no doubt paralyzed in shock as I am. We look down at a collage that may as well be an assemblage of mannequin heads. Over every picture of my dad, his face is covered with some rendition of Satan. I can't imagine how many magazines and books Mom had to scour in order to find all these varieties. Over every picture of me, my face is covered by some kind of flower, from roses to lilies to daffodils. The few pictures she has of Heidi and Bryan and all my other friends are left alone.

But what's really shocking is that pasted over every picture of her is the head of a baby. And every baby is crying.

"Ghost babies," I whisper.

"What?" Bryan turns me to him, uncertainty sheathing his face like a guise.

"The ghost babies," I repeat. "Around my junior year, Mom started mumbling about ghost babies. Only this week did I think she knew about my abortion, but clearly..." I sweep my hand over the book. "Clearly it wasn't about that. My mom thought *she* was a ghost baby." There are only a few pages left, so I hurriedly examine them. They all bear the same motif. Dad's the devil. Mom's the baby. And I'm...

All the flowers are fresh and pristine, not a single petal withered or brown.

"...And I'm the untouched flower." I stand from the book, grab my glass, and chug a huge gulp of wine, hoping it will quell the acid forming in my stomach.

"She thought I was pure." The thought is so absurd I actually laugh. I start pacing around the room, nearly tripping over all the boxes I can't seem to see because my eyes are filling up with tears. "Oh my God. She thought I was pure!" I wheel on Bryan, disgust for myself making my hands shake. "What the fuck kinda daughter was I?!" Tears slip down my cheeks and drip off my jaw. "How could I have kept something like that from her?! What was I even thinking?" I gulp more wine, hoping that by getting soused I can alleviate this gut-wrenching feeling of scumminess that sits in my chest like cancer.

"Emma, sweetie-"

"No!" I bark. "This is all my fault!" I chug, forcing down a hiccup. "Oh God! Everything I put them through! Everything I put you through! Heidi?! Since when was I such a complete and utter ass?"

I turn my back to him because I can't bear looking into his face. I'm so ashamed of myself that I wish I could just crawl into a hole and sleep for the next 100 years. The air in this house feels suddenly too thick, its mustiness encircling me and pressing me down. I gulp the rest of my wine from my glass, grab the bottle itself, and charge for the front door. I feel like I'm choking on my own contrition.

I throw open the front door and lurch down the porch steps. The air has a nip to it that I feel all the way to my bones, but I welcome it like I would a warm hug. If anyone deserves to freeze their butt off, it's me. I stand in the front yard and take a long pull from the wine bottle.

The moon is rising over the tops of the redwoods, bathing everything in a silver luminesce. The trees dance in the light, reminding me of all those sparkly dresses we used to wear to proms and formals. *Everything back then was so simple.*

I catch myself. It wasn't simple, though. My junior year was a nightmare. My senior year was a haze of dealing with the aftermath. I'll never forget the day I found out...

"Hey, Em? You doing okay? You don't look so great." Seventeen-year-old Heidi puts an arm around my shoulders.

She's right. I don't feel well. I've been nauseous all morning. I can't bring myself to eat anything. Everyone in the cafeteria is laughing and carrying on, their voices muddling together.

Bryan looks at me from across the table, concern tainting his features. I look down at the sandwich sitting untouched in front of me, the slabs of meat reminding me of those frogs we dissected in lab class last month…

Something hitches in my throat. I cover my hand over my mouth, clamping my lips shut. Oh God…I'm going to throw up!

I jolt out of my seat and run for the bathroom, the hitch in my throat getting more pronounced by the second. I don't think I'm going to make it! Oh God, oh God. I'm not going to make it!

I drop my head into the nearest garbage can and let out the contents of my stomach. Never mind that the whole cafeteria is watching me…The relief just feels so good! I feel a warm hand come to rest on my back as my retching starts to slow.

"Oh Emma," Bryan says. "You must have that flu that's going around. Come on, sweetie. Let's go to the nurse and get you home." He hands me a napkin to wipe my mouth, tucking me protectively under his arm. Concerned classmates wish me to feel better. I can't look any of them in the eyes. But I can look Heidi in the eyes, and I see the dread in her before I even register it in myself…

I take another swig of wine. Heidi had ditched classes that day and met me at my house, three pregnancy tests tucked securely into her purse. When all three came out positive, I had another gag session and cried for about two hours. When Bryan came over after school to check on me, I told him flat out that I was pregnant. He'd sat there on my bed, shocked into silence for what felt like a lifetime. I distinctly remember being the first to say I'd have an abortion. I don't think I ever asked his opinion…*Did I?*

I drop down onto the ground, the overgrown grass and weeds sticking to my bare arms.

"How could you think I was pure, Mom?" I ask the forest in front of me. "I was such a shit. I didn't think of anyone but myself." I drop my head and sob.

110

"I'm the lowest scum ever." Guilt like no other varnishes the back of my throat, leaking into my chest to coat itself closely around my heart.

"No, Em." Bryan sits down next to me. "You are not the lowest scum ever, sweetie."

"How can you possibly believe that, Bryan?" I ask around a fresh vat of tears. "I didn't even give you an option! Not with the baby, not with me leaving... Nothing!"

"Like I said before, I don't blame you for any of that, Emma." Bryan wraps me up in his arms. I don't feel like I deserve it. "Your mom thought you were pure because you *are* pure, sweetie. You have one of the best hearts I've ever known. If you didn't, I wouldn't still be in love with you." He kisses my temple. "Heidi still wouldn't love you. Steph, Kyle..." he pauses. "No one has ever loved anyone the way I love you, Emma."

I sniff, forcing myself to look into his eyes. He deserves that much.

"I love you too, Bryan," I whisper. "I never stopped."

He takes the wine bottle from my hands and gently positions me so I'm facing him. His hand cups the back of my head as he brings my mouth to his. It's such a tender kiss that fresh tears spring up behind my closed eyes. Everything I'm feeling, the sorrow, the guilt, the love, I pour into this kiss. I need Bryan to know just how much I love him, how much I've always loved him.

Under the light of the moon and with the redwood forest as our audience, we make love right there in the front yard. My eyes never leave his.

~~~

"Let's go inside," Bryan whispers. The sweat on our bodies is cooling in the night air, making me feel much colder then I should be. We unhurriedly gather up

111

our clothing. I grab the wine bottle and offer Bryan a swig, which he graciously accepts. We walk back to the house. I don't even mind that I'm buck naked.

"God, Emma. You have one of the nicest asses I've ever seen."

I laugh. "And it sounds like you've seen a few, so I'm flattered." I throw a teasing smile over my shoulder as we walk inside. Making love to Bryan was exactly what I needed to get rid of my scumminess. I feel almost light on my feet as I dump my clothes on the couch, stepping into my panties and pulling my wine-stained shirt over my head so I don't feel so bare.

"I can't bear to look at this thing anymore," I say with disgust, slamming the cover to Mom's scrapbook closed. Then I flip it over so I don't have to look at that ghastly cover. I flop onto the couch, taking the wine bottle from Bryan and drinking heavily. I don't think there's enough wine on this earth to make the crudeness of that book go away.

I watch him pull on his boxers.

"Hey...How you feel about a fire?" He asks. "I saw some wood by the side of the house this afternoon. I don't know about you but I'm not at all tired." I glance at the grandfather clock and note that it's only 9:30. I have to agree. I'm not tired at all.

"That sounds great," I say with a smile.

"Stay here. I'll be right back." He shleps out the door in just his sneakers and boxers, a vision I won't soon forget. I pull my knees up to my chest, drinking from the bottle again and then realizing it's empty.

"Easily fixable." I pop off the couch and head to the kitchen, tossing the empty bottle in the recycle bin. The Who is piping through the radio. I suddenly feel like a seeker myself as I decide on a bottle of red wine over my usual white.

I pop the cork and take the bottle back into the living room, refilling Bryan's glass as well as my own. I can hear him making his way up the porch steps, so I rush to the front door so he doesn't have to juggle an armload of wood to get inside.

As I open it, I watch his eyes turn warm as he looks me up and down. He pauses for a moment, his arm muscles straining under the weight of the wood. I know what he's thinking…How domestic this is, to have me open the door so he can build a fire. It flashes across my mind that if I did indeed stay here, this would be a regular occurrence. The idea forms a knot in my stomach and I can't decide if that knot is excitement or panic.

"Thank you, sweetie," he says as he walks past me and plants a soft kiss on my lips. The knot tightens. "More wine?" He laughs as he starts dumping logs into the fireplace.

"Hey, I plan on being blitzed for as long as I'm here. Helps with the anxiety," I add with a chuckle.

"I thought the sex was helping with that," he taunts.

"Oh, without a doubt." I smile. "Except if all I did was have sex with you, I'd get nothing done." I make my voice sound scholarly and reasonable.

"Not true." He pulls a long wooden match from the canister sitting by the fire place and strikes it. "You'd be getting *me* done."

I snort out a laugh as I take my glass and sit on the floor in front of the fireplace. The logs catch fire nicely enough, thanks to some newspaper Bryan had crunched between them. The heat feels wonderful on my bare legs. I close my eyes and breathe in heavily. I've always loved this smell. It brings me back to the many Christmases here where I'd been too excited to sleep and had to wake my parents up before the sun rose. Dad would amble downstairs to build a fire while I'd snuggle in bed with Mom and she'd tell me stories about hearing sleigh bells at night. The memory makes me smile.

See? Not all bad.

113

I open my eyes and watch Bryan sit down across from me, Indian style. *Not bad at all.*

"I still want to look at those letters addressed to my dad, but I don't think I can handle any more revelations tonight."

"I can't say I blame you," Bryan says with a laugh. "We can tackle that tomorrow. Just like the books."

I smile graciously. And with that we spend the rest of the evening sipping wine.

Chapter 11

At some point last night, Bryan and I migrated up to my bedroom. I don't really remember because once we finished the bottle of red wine, I was pretty sufficiently sauced. Being sauced, however, did not keep the demons at bay. I tossed and turned all night, dreaming of babies and devils and hearing a high, melancholy whimper every time I woke up. Too late did I realize that sound was me. My only salve was Bryan, who would pull me protectively up against his chest.

A lugubrious cloud has settled over me this morning. Maybe it's because of the scrapbook. Maybe it's because I'm finally getting rid of this house's contents. Or maybe it's because once this house is empty, there's no real reason for me to stay.

I'm standing in the shower, wishing the water would wash away my blues. I can hear Bryan shaving at the sink, humming a tune I can't place. It's so…homey, having him here while I shower. And afterward, I have no doubt we will head downstairs for some breakfast, then wait for Heidi to show up so we can get all the furniture I'll be keeping out into the U-Haul. Then the Red Cross will show up, take everything else away, and that will be it.

My stomach clenches.

"Hey, Em. What time did you say the Red Cross was showing up?"

Bryan's voice startles me out of my thoughts.

"Oh. Um...I think, ten?" It comes out as a question because I'm still distracted with my clenched tummy.

"Okay, good. We've got some time then."

It's early, just a little after eight. After all my fitful dreams last night, it seemed a waste to just lie in bed and stew over them.

I rinse the conditioner from my hair, willing my blues to go down the drain with it. I turn off the water, giving off a surprised laugh as a bath towel magically appears from over the curtain rod.

"Thank you," I giggle. I towel off as best I can and open the curtain. Bryan is leaning against the counter, arms crossed over his bare chest and a contented smile gracing his face as he watches me step out of the tub.

"This is nice, Em. I mean, starting the mornings with you."

"Yes it is," I squeak out.

"Will you stay?"

I smile down at my feet. Bryan was right: he is selfish enough to ask me to stay. He asked me once last night as we were crawling into bed and all I could do was snuggle up under his arm and close my eyes. He knows I don't have an answer for that, but I think he believes that if he asks enough times, he'll eventually wear me down. Clever tactic, because my nerve is waning as I watch him watch me start to dress in cut-off shorts and a tank top.

Surprisingly, the sun is shining this morning, the temperature a balmy 70 degrees, a rarity for the likes of summer in Eureka. And given that it's already this

115

warm this early in the morning, I anticipate a very sweaty day hauling furniture and boxes around.

"Let's get some breakfast," I use as my answer. I wrap an arm around his waist and guild him down the hall. And God bless him, he doesn't push the topic.

I go about brewing a pot of coffee and Bryan starts making some eggs and toast. I turn on the stereo, happy to hear The Hollies singing about a long, cool woman. When I was a kid, every time this song came on I envisioned myself as this long, cool woman. I'd picture myself in a flowing red dress, my long blonde hair artfully disheveled. It would appear as if I'd just woken from a nap, but since I was so beautiful, it didn't matter that I'd just woken from a nap. Oh, the naiveté of children.

"When's Heidi getting here?" Bryan asks. He's whisking the eggs together in the large salad bowl I will be taking home with me. The movement is so rhythmic I find my tongue halfway tied.

"Um...soon-ish. I think." I suspect that the bad dreams are affecting my brain. I've felt off all morning...Or maybe it's that blasted scrapbook. I can feel its presence from the living room all the way over here in the kitchen. Maybe I should burn it...

I give myself a little shake.

Pull it together, Em.

When breakfast is ready, we eat together at the dining room table, sharing our one plate and one fork. At least I had the state of mind to keep a few coffee mugs.

I'm just rinsing up the dishes when Heidi comes bursting through the front door.

"I'm here!" She hollers in her sing-song voice. Despondent mood aside, it still makes me smile.

"In the kitchen!" Bryan hollers back.

"Well isn't this just the picture-perfect rendition of a 1940's household," she jabs laughingly. I can't hold the chuckle in because it's damned true. Little wifey, standing at the sink doing dishes as big, strong hubby expertly moves boxes around the kitchen and dining room, organizing for the movers. My gut clenches tighter.

"How was the rest of last night?" She asks.

I glance over my shoulder and give her a sly smile. She affords me with a wink.

"God, girls really do share everything, don't they?" Bryan cavils.

"A fact all men need to come to terms with," Heidi says prissily.

"Actually, last night was a bit of an eye-opener. Go into the living room and check out that scrapbook we found yesterday," I say. "It's on the coffee table."

She drops her purse on the kitchen counter and makes towards the living room. One kitchen box has been left open so I start to load up the rest of the kitchenware I won't be keeping.

About three minutes goes by when I hear, "What the shit?! Emma! What the hell is this?!" Heidi's holding the book in her arms to one of the pages featuring Dad as the devil. Shock and something akin to terror shines from her eyes.

"Oh, it gets better," I say dryly. "Keep looking."

"I'm not sure I want to," she says under her breath, but like the BFF she is, she continues to leaf through the pages. I hear her breath hitch as she comes upon the crying babies, the flowers, the totally random pictures that don't hold any kind of storyline. When she comes to the end of the book, she slaps it shut, drops it on the kitchen counter and rushes to the sink.

"I feel like I need to wash my hands," she grumbles.

"Pretty twisted, right?"

"What does it all mean? I mean, clearly she was not too fond of your dad, but..."

"Remember how she talked about ghost babies?"

Understanding lights up Heidi's eyes. "Oh, shit."

"And notice how all the flowers over my face are all fresh and pure?"

Her brow wrinkles as she considers this. I glance over at Bryan and see that he's stopped organizing to watch our exchange. He gives me a small wink and my stomach clenches further still.

"Oh God," Heidi breathes after a few moments. "She thought you were a virgin."

"Or something close to that," I say. "She obviously didn't know about junior year. Which makes me feel like the biggest heel in the world."

"Why does that make you feel like a heel? I thought you didn't want her to know?"

I huff as I wring my hands through a kitchen towel...decorated with red poppies. My mind conjures up my dream and I instantly drop it on the counter.

"Because...I dunno. It just does. Like, I kept this gigantic secret from my mother. My mother! A secret that damn near killed me. And all that time she thought I was just this innocent little girl..." I can feel my eyes starting to tear up again so I resume my task of packing up the rest of the kitchen. "It just reaffirms the fact that I was a selfish jerk."

"Oh my freaking God, you have *got* to get off of that," Heidi exclaims. "You weren't selfish, babe. You were young. You dealt with the situation the best way you knew how." She says this as she wraps me in a hug.

Her words make me feel marginally better. After all, if Heidi and Bryan can forgive me for all my shortcomings, I should be able to forgive myself, right?

118

"Okay…Enough of this heavy shit. We've got enough going on today without adding in some self-condemnation," Bryan says as he enters the kitchen and gives my temple a light kiss. "How about we load up the U-Haul with everything you're keeping, Em. And Heidi, you said you're keeping the china cabinet, right?" She nods. "Perfect. We'll get it in the van and drive it to your place this afternoon, once the movers are gone. Then we're going to dinner and then I'm taking Emma back here to convince her to stay with me."

Heidi starts laughing and I can't help but smile and roll my eyes because that is indeed what Bryan will do.

~~~

Watching the movers take my parents' stuff away is amazingly gut-wrenching. I didn't realize how attached I was to the couch, the chairs, the beds, but as it turns out, with each item being stashed into their moving van, I find a few new tears break from their flimsy barrier. I've got the grandfather clock, mom's desk and hope chest stashed safely away in my little U-Haul, along with Heidi's china cabinet. We've also stashed away the few boxes of mementos I'm keeping. The only things not in the U-Haul are the scrapbook, the box of *The Bell Jar*s and Dad's letters.

As much as I want to burn the scrapbook, I can't bring myself to do it. It's a queer souvenir to keep, but I can't seem to help myself. The movers almost got away with Mom's box of *The Bell Jar*s, but luckily I was able to save it in time. Again, I'm not sure why I want to keep a whole case of this book, but I do. Maybe now I'm the one going crazy…?

I help carry box after box out to the Red Cross truck and each seems to get a little heavier as the house becomes lighter. I know I'm doing the right thing, but it's still heartbreaking.

Bryan and Heidi leave me to wallow in my own thoughts, for which I'm eternally grateful. They don't try to make light of the situation because they know it's not a light situation. I'm clearing out my childhood home; all these memories are going to be scattered to other families around Humboldt. And I can only freaking hope that these items, however small they may be, will bring someone joy the way they did me when I was a kid.

It takes the three of us and two other professional movers five hours to clear out the house. I'm not sure if this is good timing or not, but as I stand on the porch flanked by Bryan and Heidi, I suddenly feel as if all the bones have been extracted from my body. We watch the truck make a wide turn and amble down the long driveway, its sides getting scratched by the very branches that had grazed my van just a few days ago. A lump the size of Mount Vesuvius has formed in my throat and I have to bite my knuckles to keep from sobbing.

"It'll be okay, Em," Bryan says as he wraps an arm around my shoulders.

All I can do is nod.

"Okay…I have an idea," Heidi says, turning me to face her. Her eyes roam my face like she's searching for something. When she finds it she gives me a gentle smile.

"Right. How about this? Maybe Bryan could take me in the U-Haul to drop off my new cabinet and you can stay here and just have some alone time. Then Bryan and I can grab some grub from somewhere and bring it back and we can all have a little picnic out here on the porch. It's such a beautiful day and we pasty-pale Eureka folk need extra vitamin D whenever we can get it."

120

I don't know how she does it. I really don't. It's like a golden cord connects her brain to mine and any time that cord vibrates with my substantial agitation, she comes to my rescue like a knight on a white steed. It's unprecedented. I give her a wavering smile as fresh tears pool at the corners of my eyes.

Bryan, also true to form, catches on without a hitch.

"Great idea, Heidi." I feel him give my shoulder a squeeze before he goes inside to get the keys to the van.

"Thank you," I whisper.

"What are sisters for?" She gives me a wink along with a fierce hug that lasts until Bryan comes back.

"We'll be back soon, sweetie." He gives me a kiss that could end all kisses. It's almost like he's trying to milk my grief out through my mouth and I think my heart explodes a little at the gesture.

They get into the U-Haul and give me big, goofy waves as they drive off.

My body sinks to the top step of the porch. I drop my head in my hands, letting my hair fan down to cover my face. The tears come without preamble. They are big and wet and I don't bother trying to wipe them from my face. I'm shocked at how much this process has hurt me, seeing all my parents stuff carted away. I mean, I knew it was coming, I just didn't realize how hard it would be. It feels good to cry, though, like I'm somehow becoming whole again by letting myself feel the grief of everything I left behind.

I sit here for quite some time, until my tears dry up and my bones come back into my body.

I ease off the step and turn towards the door that I forgot to shut. It gapes at me, taunting me to enter a house that is now devoid of personality, of life.

"Don't be a baby, Emma," I chide myself. "It's still your house." I square my shoulders and walk through the door. My ears are assaulted with the thump-

121

thump of my own footsteps. They echo throughout the empty space, only adding fuel to the proverbial fire.

"You had to do it. You can't stay here."

Silence.

"New York is your home now, damnit."

"You can't very well give up everything you have there. Not for this." My hand sweeps out.

"It's still your house."

"God, you need a freaking distraction."

The box of books is sitting in the living room with the scrapbook and letters on top of it. Anything is better than this silence. I march over to the stereo, which we turned off when the movers arrive. I flick it to life. Herman's Hermits serenade me. I guess I'm not getting any milk today.

I plop down in the middle of the living room and open the box. Dozens of copies of *The Bell Jar* look up at me. It's so peculiar that Mom would purchase a case of these...Then again, it's not like she was right in the head by that point. I eye the scrapbook with distain. Clearly she had issues. Even still, my heart weeps at what she had to go through. She and my dad both.

I have no idea what he did to piss her off so much, but clearly it was enough to send her over the edge. I'm curious as to why they didn't just get a divorce after I went away to college. Why stick it out and be miserable together?

I lift a copy of the book from the box and thumb through it. I had thought that these books were untouched, but this one has a giant "ONE" written across the back cover and a few of the page numbers have been circled.

"That's odd," I say to the room.

I pick up a second book and go to the back of the cover and, sure enough, there's a "THREE" written in my mother's loopy handwriting. Again, a few page numbers have been circled. I cross-reference and note that these are different from the first book. I start pulling book after book from the box. Every single one is numbered, all twenty-three of them, an odd number in my opinion. And every single one has different page numbers circled.

I stack the books according to the numbers on the back and sit Indian style, simply staring at them.

"What were you doing, Mom?"

The house groans in response. Despite today's heat, a trill runs up and down my back, like someone is blowing cool air on my spine.

"Oh!" I practically spring off the floor and run up to my room.

"I completely forgot about the other book!" The one I found in Mom's room makes the case of books an even twenty-four. I extract it from my suitcase, along with Mom's worn copy and head back downstairs, the notion of a possible mission giving my step a little more bounce. I flip to the back of the black-covered one, not at all surprised to see a large "TWENTY-FOUR" written on it.

I sit back down and add the last book to the pile, setting Mom's worn copy on top of my little pillar like a sacrificial offering. All I can do is stare at it.

"It's gotta mean something. I mean, really…What was she trying to say?"

My eyes drift to the window. Sunlight streams through the redwood forest, casting eccentric shadows across the ground. A light breeze has picked up, making the branches dance. On impulse I go to the window and open it, feeling the need for some fresh air across my face. And I really don't care that it's not even four o'clock yet. I go to the kitchen and open a bottle of white wine, pleased with myself for having the foresight to not pack away the wine glasses or the bottle opener. I pour myself a large glass and go back to the living room.

"I'm gonna figure this out if it kills me."

I pick up Mom's book, the very first copy that I'd discovered in her library, and leaf through it. A number of words and phrases have been highlighted throughout the entire book. I notice the highlighter marks are somewhat faded with age. *She must have done this a while ago...Like maybe when I was in high school..?*

I glance at the neat stack of books sitting in front of me. An idea starts to form in my mind. I reach into my purse and pull out a little notepad and a pen. I'm not even sure where this idea comes from, but as if blown in on a breeze scented with the aroma of redwoods, it coils itself around my brain like a snake. And before I let my better half talk me out of it, I grab the "ONE" book from the pile and leaf through it, taking note of all the pages that are circled. There are only a couple. I reference the numbers in my mother's worn book, writing down the words that are highlighted on the proper pages.

What I come up with makes my stomach drop into hell and the hair on the back of my neck stand erect as razor blades.

"TO MY DAUGHTER."

"Oh my God." Something akin to ice forms in my veins as I realize what this is. "She left me a message." As if in answering, a swift breeze blows through the open window, stirring my hair and, despite the warmth of the day, chilling me down to the bone.

"She must have spent...I don't know...a long time...doing this." I have no idea what to think.

"I wish I knew when she did this!" Silence answers me.

"I've gotta find out what she said!"

A frenzy wants to take over my body, but I know I need to keep my cool. If I miss any circled pages, I won't get the entirety of the message. I look through book "ONE" once more, making sure that pages 150 and 198 are the only ones circled. When I'm satisfied, I place it delicately to the side and reach for book "TWO." I

124

sift through and see that pages 32, 69, and 140 are circled. All other pages are left alone. I'm actually somewhat terrified to see what I'll decipher, but I can't stop now. Mom did all this so that I would find something out, something big enough that her unwell mind concocted a sort of game out of it.

I reference her book.

My heart sinks.

I actually feel my chest constrict as I register what she's telling me.

"YOUR FATHER...HAD AN AFFAIR...I PAUSED IN THE DOORWAY OF THE LIVING ROOM."

"No...no...Oh, God." The pen slips from my hand as I go to clutch my stomach. *Dad had an affair?! What the hell!* That can't be possible. *Dad was so loyal! He would never do something like that!*

"Cleary, he did, Emma! Why else would Mom suddenly go down the tubes!?"

I forage my brain to try and remember when exactly they started acting differently towards each other. It was definitely my junior year. I know that much because I had the abortion after Christmas, and that was when all hell seemed to break lose.

"There's only one way to find out, Emma." With a shaky hand, I pick up my pen, make sure book "TWO" is accounted for, and move on to book "THREE." Pages 87, 134, and 196 are circled.

"IT WAS THE DAY AFTER CHRISTMAS...THE TEARS CAME IN A RUSH...I SAID, 'THE DEVIL.'"

"Oh my freaking God," I exclaim to the book in front of me. "Dad cheated on Mom the day after Christmas." It all makes sense now, timeline-wise. And it also explains why Dad's head is covered in all those devil pictures in the scrapbook. My heart breaks.

"Oh, Dad. What did you get yourself into?"

I go through book after book and piece together the message Mom left for me, all the while feeling like my heart may shatter. She felt deserted and yet my dad still hoped that everything would be okay between them. I guess he'd hoped she could get past his infidelity. What a fool!

I'm not sure how much more I can handle. I'm at book "SIXTEEN" and I feel like my internals are going to come up through my mouth. They almost do, in fact, when I piece together the next part of the message.

"THE BABY...YOUR FATHER'S...I SAW THE BABY COMING OUT...A TINY CURLED-UP BODY THE SIZE OF A FROG...IT WENT IN A BOTTLE."

The image is so revolting that I toss down the book and run for the bathroom, just barely making it to the toilet before the meager contents in my stomach make their return. I heave until there's nothing left. And even then, I feel like more may come up.

Dad had gotten another woman pregnant. And since my mom refused to give up her few shifts at the hospital...

"Jesus...She saw the whole thing," I say into the toilet.

She must have been keeping tabs on whomever this woman was and when Mom found out she went into labor, she took a shift at the hospital...*No wonder she didn't want to give up her job!*

I can't imagine what that would have been like: To see the woman your husband had an affair with give birth to a stillborn. And Mom had always talked about how she'd wished she could have given me a sibling...

I rest my head on my hands, leaning heavily on the seat of the toilet. I want to cry, but I feel it won't do any good. Clearly, what's done is done. What I can do now is finish this message and give my mother the valediction she deserves, madness be damned.

I ease off the floor, rinse my mouth out with some water, and make my way back towards the living room. My legs and hands won't stop shaking, so I use the wall as my guide. These walls that have seen so much…

"Pull it together, Em. For Mom."

That thought allows me to take a few deep breaths.

I ease back down onto the floor, take a small sip of wine, and make sure "SIXTEEN" is covered.

Book "NINETEEN" almost makes me throw up again.

"I BURIED IT…IN THE WOODS BY THE FROZEN PONDS… RINGED BY A RED BRICK WALL."

"Oh Christ," I moan. "Mom…Oh, God, Mom."

Since Mom was a nurse, she had access to all those stillborns.

She stole it.

She stole the freaking baby!

I don't know what to do with myself. I grab my wine and get up off the floor. I walk towards the window and just stare at the sunlight streaming through the trees.

"The woods by the frozen ponds…" My mind flashes to my dream, watching my mother troll through the redwood forest with a bundle in her arms…Bryan seeing her the day I told him I was leaving. Again, timeline-wise, it's seamless.

A lightbulb goes off.

"Oh shit! She's talking about that little patch of water we have on our property! The pond that freezes over during really cold winters!" I smack my hand against my head. "Of course!"

127

I want to run out the door and see if this is, in fact, true, but I can't abandon my project just yet. I need to find out what else she wanted me to know. I spend another minute letting all of this new information seep in before I return to deciphering the rest of the books. She clearly loathed my father for what he did. I can't say I blame her.

By the time I get to book "TWENTY-FOUR," I'm so depressed that the thought of cutting my own wrists doesn't sound half bad. My father was the reason for Mom's decline. Not me, not my own issues, but something he did years ago that broke her. I flip through the book, but only come across one page that was circled. Page 237.

"WE'LL ACT AS IF ALL THIS WAS A BAD DREAM."

Chapter 12

A tear slips down my cheek and falls onto Mom's book.

"She tried to act as if nothing happened for my sake." Obviously, she didn't say this outright, but the implication is clear. She tried to protect me, her pure little child, by acting like nothing had happened. But all the while, it ate at her until her mind simply snapped.

"Jesus Christ," I moan into my hands. "Why did all this happen?!" I scream into the house. "Fuck!"

I want so badly to just drink my sorrows away, but I can't do that. Not yet anyways. I have a puzzle to solve. And I know the only way I'll find out is by keeping my head on straight.

Why did this happen?

I let the question roll around in my brain. Yet another breeze blows in through the open window, ruffling the pages of Mom's book.

"Oh shit! The letters!" How had I not thought of them until now? *Of course!* I scramble across the floor and clutch them to my chest.

They feel like they're radiating a truth I'm sure will only depress me further, but I owe it to Mom to find out. And, I suppose, I owe it to Dad. Even though he cheated on her and got some woman pregnant, I can't seem to hate him the way

Mom did. I'm disappointed and heartsick, obviously, but I'm not mad. I'm just confused.

"These will rectify that." I scuttle back to my little nest amongst Mom's books. I untie the twine that's wrapped around the letters and let it flutter to the floor. I note that there are a total of five letters and, coincidentally, all are numbered in my mother's distinctive writing at the bottom right-hand corner.

"So you were banking on me finding these, right? And you wanted to make sure I read them in order?" A light breeze rustles my hair in answering.

"You have such pretty hair, Emma," Mom says to my twelve-year-old self. "How about you let me braid it?"

I smile that awkward preteen, goofy grin and scamper across the couch to sit on the floor in front of my mother. She magically produces a brush, as if from out of thin air, and starts a slow stroke from the roots of my hair all the way down to the tips that hit just below my shoulder blades. My eyes inadvertently close and I savor the feel of someone playing with my hair.

"You are such girls," Dad laughs from the reading chair by the fireplace. He lowers his paper and stares at us. "How I did it is anyone's guess."

"How you did what, honey?" I can hear the smile in my mom's voice.

"How I managed to get the two most beautiful girls and keep a hold of them, that's what."

"You're so silly, Dad." I say this without opening my eyes, but my chest inflates slightly at being called beautiful.

"Ron, I think we're all pretty lucky."

The Drifters pull me back from the memory. I suddenly wish I were under a boardwalk right now, away from all this drama, all these macabre and dispiriting realizations about my family that I was either too self-absorbed to notice or that they just did a damned good job keeping from me. At this point it doesn't really matter.

130

I don't recognize the writing on the envelopes, but that's not horribly surprising. I extract the first letter from the first envelope, not even realizing I'm holding my breath until I feel my lungs start to burn.

"Stop being so dramatic, Em," I say in a puff of air.

The letter is folded neatly into thirds. Based off the worn creases, I can tell it's been read a number of times, by either my dad or my mother or both still remains a mystery.

As I unfold the paper, I let my eyes blur so that the words won't stand out to me just yet. I do notice that the penmanship is very lady-like, all cursive and blue-ribbon. It certainly puts my mother's questionable scrawl into perspective.

As I re-focus my eyes, I note the date at the top of the letter: December 13th, 2008. My timeline is confirmed...It did, indeed, start my junior year.

The greeting squeezes my heart.

My Dearest Ronald,

It was so wonderful to meet you this past weekend. By the way...I hope you don't mind, but I got your address from Principal Howard. (The principal from the high school?!)

That conference would have been a real bore without your stellar personality to make it more exciting!

Listen...I know that you felt something the way I felt something. I could tell in the way you looked at me. (Brazen bitch!) *I could tell in the way we shared those dances.*

I know you're married and I respect the institution of marriage. (Clearly not!) *But I was wondering if perhaps we could meet for a drink?*

I'd love to pick your brain about World War I, since that obviously seems to be your favorite war to analyze. (Stop pretending like you know him!) *And since I'm writing my dissertation on it, maybe you could help me with some of the gaps I need to fill.* (Gap, my ass! You want him to fill something else!)

Anyway, I hope I hear from you soon!

Take care,

Love. (Love?!)

Kimberly Hutcherson

"Fucking Ms. Hutcherson?! The history teacher?!" I scream at the room. I remember that she came to teach at the high school at the beginning of my freshman year. She was attractive, no doubt about that. And since she and Dad were both history teachers, they must have become friends...Attended a conference together...Felt a little spark. I loath the idea, but facts are facts, I guess.

I have no idea if Dad slept with her just the one time, but obviously it was enough to get her pregnant.

And since I was dealing with all of my own issues after junior year, I barely registered her swollen belly. Even though, as I remember now with a start, it was top gossip around school. That year, everyone was asking: "Who knocked up Ms Hutcherson?"

How self-absorbed was I!?

"Em? Are you okay?" Bryan's concerned voice drifts towards me from the entryway, momentary dousing the fire that's burning in my veins. Again, I'm not necessarily mad at my father. I'm more angry with this slut who thought it was okay to take a run at a married man.

I look up as Bryan and Heidi enter the living room, Bryan carrying two large bags, the smell of Chinese food reminding me that I haven't eaten much today and what I did eat, I threw up not too long ago. The look on my face must read like a horror movie because they both stop dead in their tracks once they see me.

"Em, what's going on?" Heidi's eyes roam over the stacks of books scattered around me, the letters sitting at my side, the dreaded scrapbook that started this whole fiasco. Her voice is cautionary, like she's talking to a skittish pony...or a lunatic. I probably look the part with my tear-streaked face and disheveled hair.

"Boy, have you two missed some good, clean fun!" I say with a sarcastic snort. "As it turns out, my mother left me a cryptic note using all these books to tell me that my father had an affair." I can't keep the acid out of my voice.

"What?!" They exclaim in unison.

"Oh yeah. It gets better, though. Not only did he have an affair with Ms. Hutcherson, the history teacher—" I wave the letter for emphasis. "—He also got her pregnant."

Based off their gaping mouths, I can tell I've shocked them into silence. I use this silence to fill them in on how Mom left me her message. I read it to them and feel the air get heavier with desolation. I then read them the first letter from Kimberly. I'm not sure I want to read the rest of them, but I know that my own curiosity will get the better of me.

In the end, we read the rest of the letters together, Heidi by my side and me nestled between Bryan's legs, his chest pressing into my back like a supportive pillar. Heidi's hand rests lightly on my knee, giving it the occasional squeeze when we come across something particularly crippling in Kimberly's letters.

Indeed, my father did meet her for drinks. He did, in fact, fuck her and get her pregnant.

The third letter confirms that my father didn't want to be with her, based on how acidly it reads. But she'd already decided to keep the baby, so there was no turning back.

By the time we've finished reading the last letter, I'm so nauseous even the smell of the Chinese food makes bile rise in my throat. I remove myself from the floor and go to stand at the window, hoping a little fresh air will temper the churning of my stomach.

"It's no wonder my father started drinking so much," I say to no one in particular. "She was basically threatening his job. Then she threatened to tell Mom when he wouldn't budge." I hang my head. "Not that it mattered much in the end...Mom still found out about the baby." I pause. "The baby! Oh God! I have to go find it!"

I rush for the front door, but then I'm stopped by an iron-clad hand on my arm. I look up into Bryan's sympathetic eyes and it makes me want to cry all the more.

"Emma, is that really such a good idea?" He asks gently.

"Yes! I need to see for myself. I need to make sure."

I extract my arm from his hand. "I know what you're thinking. You must think I'm completely insane." I laugh. "Hell, maybe I am. The apple never falls too far from the tree, does it?"

Bryan's brow furrows. I see Heidi get up from the floor, anxiety written across her face like a poem. I can't help the hysterical cackle that pops out of my mouth.

"I knew this would happen. I knew I was going down the rabbit hole the second I crossed the Humboldt County line." More laughter. "Can't fight the inevitable, right?"

"Emma— "

I cut Bryan off with a sharp shake of my head.

"I have to do this," I say, a little more harshly than intended.

I'm afraid he's going to see the crazy in my eyes, so I whirl away from him and sprint out the front door. I have no idea if they will follow me, but I'm too task-driven to look back and check. I pump my legs and charge through the overgrown and scraggy front yard. The heat of the day hasn't dissipated, even though the sun is starting her slow decent behind the tree line. I instantly feel sweat break out across my brow. I crash into the redwood forest and it's like my childhood comes rushing back to me, directing me where to go even though I haven't explored these woods in over a decade. It's almost as if I can feel the paper wings on my back, fluttering in the wind and carrying me away.

The trails Heidi and I carved from years of exploring have been overgrown with time, but that only makes me more determined to find my destination. I run until my legs burn and my lungs catch a certain fire that I almost relish in.

I remember the pond Mom is referring to as more of a slough of water that just happened to freeze over during the winter. Heidi and I would pretend-ice-skate on it. It wasn't more then a few feet deep, but it was large enough to allow substantial playtime.

I don't, however, remember a red brick wall. I have to wonder if Mom constructed that as some kind of shrine to this baby that she stole.

As I get closer to my destination, I slow my pace to a brisk walk. I don't want to miss any details. My ragged breathing starts to slow and since I'm no longer listening to myself pounding through the foliage, I can now appreciate the little chirps and twitters from the birds perched high within the redwood forest. It reminds me of my dream, seeing my father hanging from that noose. A shudder wracks my body and the sweat now running freely down my face and spine turns cold.

"You really did dig your own grave, Dad."

I slow my pace as the familiar sound of gently running water adds to the cacophony of noises surrounding me. I'd forgotten our property also has a little creek that runs through it, just another added bonus for mine and Heidi's playtime back in the day.

Through the light and shadows I can make out the pond. It's smaller than I remember it. It's also dirtier. God only knows what bacteria is growing in there. It's only slightly jarring to see this place again, but what really gets the hair on my neck to stand up is the little brick wall that sits on the far side of the pond.

"I definitely don't remember that from when I was a kid."

I slow my pace even more. I take a moment before I make my way around the pond to look up into the forest canopy, admiring the arrant size and enormity of the trees surrounding me.

"You are home, Emma. You know that, right?"

"Yes."

"Even after everything you've just discovered, even after going over there and confirming what's already likely true, you know you won't leave."

"Yes."

"You know your life is here, with Bryan and Heidi and Steph and everyone else."

"Yes."

"I think you can well and truly say you're fucked."

"Yes."

I heave a sigh. In validating what I'd been dreading since driving here, in surrendering to what I've been fighting, it's a relief to finally admit the truth: I'm home.

I watch my footing as I start to walk around the pond towards the wall, careful not to slip and ruin my shoes in water that can only be described as sludge.

As I get closer, I notice the bricks are worn down, no doubt from years of elemental torture. It's a small little wall, maybe a few feet high and perhaps three feet long. It's not so much a wall, really, as it is a stack of bricks. My mother was clearly not into masonry. I'm not entirely sure what I expect to see as I come around the side of the wall. Do I expect to see the skeletal remains of a fetus? Bloody clothes? Some kind of tomb signifying the death of something so innocent and yet conceived in sin?

So I'm oddly disappointed when I look and find nothing. The ground is strewn with leaves from the redwoods, sticks and not much else.

"This isn't right. There has to be something."

"I BURIED IT," she'd said

But obviously Mom didn't go for fanfare when she buried the baby, because not even a pebble indicates where she may have interred it.

I drop to my knees and start digging with my hands. Twigs scratch at my exposed knees and it's not long before my well-manicured nails are chipped, soil encrusted all along their beds. Sweat reemerges on my brow, trickling down between my breasts and pooling at the small of my back. I don't let the uncomfortable sensations stop me, though.

I dig and dig and dig. It feels like I dig forever. Luckily for me, the soil is so soft with moisture that it's not horribly difficult to create a rather large hole.

I nearly gasp when my fingers finally stroke across something solid. I brush some of the dirt from the exposed surface. It's clearly a canister of some sort. My morbid excitement spurs me on. I dig faster, finding the edges and trying to get a good grip so I can pry it from its shallow grave.

It's unceremonious, pulling this thing from the ground. No angels sing, no seraphic light shines down on me like you see in the movies. I just pull the canister from the dirt and gently try to wipe off years of grime. It's light, barely ten pounds. The top is sealed shut and I rather prefer it that way. God knows I don't need to be opening this thing to see what's inside. I just needed confirmation that this is, in fact, my half sibling. That Mom was telling the truth.

Something like peace washes over me.

"This is all I need to know."

I hug it to my chest. I feel a connection to it that I can't quite describe, a weird, tenuous link to the baby I also lost.

"I get it now, Mom. I get why everything happened to you."

Then the lightbulb goes off.

"She was jealous…"

Of course!

Mom always wanted another baby, that was no secret.

No doubt she felt betrayed by Dad, but what's more was that she envied Kimberly, to even have the ability to reproduce. That would be enough to drive someone crazy, in my opinion. After all, didn't I, after my abortion, go a little insane also?

And didn't Bryan, like my dad, try to placate the beast, but to no avail?

So Dad did the only thing he thought to do…Drink.

I look up into the brise-soleil formed by the branches, imagining that my father is no longer dangling from a rope of his own making. I imagine him coming down and coming to rest beside me.

"I'm not mad at you, Dad."

I picture him smiling and it's almost like I can feel decades of grief wash off of me as I finally come to peace with this place, this town, the unfortunate turn my family took, the unfortunate turn *I* took.

I look down at the container in my hands. I turn it over, giving it a once-over. I notice words scribbled across the surface, but under all the grime, it's hard to make them out. I glance at the pond and let the idea carry my feet over to the edge of the water. It may be murky and disgusting, but it is wet.

I place the canister in my lap as I kneel down and cup my hands at the waters edge. Using them as a ladle, I pour the water over the tin, scrubbing gently with my fingers.

A contented smile forms across my lips as the words "BELL-HUTCHER-SON" appear before my eyes. A small breath leaves my body.

"It was an ill-conceived idea, certainly, but you will always be my sibling."

Chapter 13

I'm making my way back towards home, a tranquil trek compared to the manic sprint I made not too long ago.

I reburied the container and even went so far as to make a sort of teepee-like structure on top of it, complete with some wildflowers I picked in a nearby field. I know one swift rainfall will completely dismantle my work, but it makes me feel better knowing I paid tribute to what would have been my baby sister or brother. I kind of wish I knew what the sex of the baby was, but I guess it's a shade fitting that I don't, given everything else my parents kept from me all these years…Everything I kept from them…

Maybe it's the fact that I know now, but that contented sensation has only bloomed brighter within me. I know why Mom went off her rocker and I know why Dad became an alcoholic. The mysteries of my family's downfall have finally been unveiled and though it still clenches my heart to see a once happy unit crack, I can finally lay all those questions to rest. And I can finally accept that it wasn't my own stupidity that made it happen. That may sound horribly selfish, but no child wants to be responsible for her parents' undoing.

I walk slowly and with a purpose. The temperature has finally started to drop now that the sun is below the trees, and I welcome the cool kiss across my hot skin. Through the branches, I can see the sky turning a beautiful shade of coral. The sunset tonight should be spectacular from the second-story deck...Perhaps we will enjoy our Chinese food from there.

I break through the barrier of the trees and see Bryan and Heidi sitting on the steps of my house. Gratitude for them not pursuing me, rather, letting me make this closure on my own, overwhelms me.

When they see me, they both stand. I watch as Heidi places her hand on Bryan's shoulder and says something I can't hear. But I can guess what it is.

A huge smile breaks across my face. And when I start running towards him, he starts an elegant gallop that takes me right into his arms. His heart pounds turbulently against mine as our lips meet in a kiss that, without words, seals the proverbial deal.

"Anywhere with you," I whisper against his mouth. He clutches me closer to his body, giving off a shuddering laugh.

"Anywhere with you."

The redwood forest applauds us.

Epilogue

I close my laptop and sit back in my chair, rolling my shoulders a few times to work out the kinks.

"Revisions really are no fun," I say to the empty room. I glance out the window and watch as the forest sits dormant, basking in the light coat of rain that started this morning. Normally this type of weather would have depressed me, but I find the pitter-patter across the rooftop calmative, like white noise or one of those meditative apps I'm constantly trying to get Heidi to use. This white noise is blending well with The Five Americans, who apparently "see the light."

It took me long enough, but finally, I do too...

With a slight jolt, I realize something. This song hit number twenty-six on the Top 40 list in 1966. I'm twenty-six, seeing the light for the first time every since I pieced together Mom's message. Pride and something akin to gratitude flowers within me.

I stand, moving behind my desk chair, and arch my back. I've been sitting pretty much all day.

"I think I deserve a break."

I lean over my desk to save the progress I've made and power down my computer, switching off my little radio as well.

The small bump in my belly brushes the back of my chair, a gentle reminder that eventually I won't be able to bend over to tie my own shoes. The thought makes me softly laugh.

I rest my hand over this little bump, only now starting to show. At first I was worried that something was wrong, that somehow my own uterus had killed the fetus even before it started to grow. But my OB-GYN reassured me, numerous times, that because this is my first pregnancy (to term, that is), I won't show for at least three to four months. Once I thought I was starting to show the creation of my and Bryan's union, I've made Bryan measure my stomach every week to confirm that, yes, the baby is still strong and growing.

I don't care if that makes me paranoid: I'm doing everything in my power to not screw this up.

I close the door to my office (formally my parents' room—the ghosts no longer live there) and start to make my way downstairs, feeling the urge for a steaming cup of hot chocolate. I've been pregnant now for just under fifteen weeks and thus far, the cravings haven't been as bad as I'd originally anticipated. Hot chocolate is high on the list, as are oranges (weird, I know) and, even weirder, kale. Bryan says it's because I'm unconsciously instilling healthy habits into our baby, but I'm thinking it's more my long lineage of wackiness. It does beat the usual cravings of ice cream and chips, a bullet my hips and thighs are happy we dodged.

As I make my way downstairs, it still manages to blow my mind wide open that I would, in fact, want to keep this home that has housed so many distressing

142

memories. But, at the end of the day, it seemed the pleasant far surpassed the unpleasant. I could get rid of my parents' belongings, their furniture, everything that made this house theirs, but I couldn't bring myself to disengage from the actual house itself. And since it's now infused with my and Bryan's belongings, the past seems irrelevant at this point.

It's not just the house, though...It's also the property.

I take a moment in the dining room to stare out the window. These woods are indeed the inspiration for my children's book, after all. How could I possibly give that up?

I'm not sure how it never occurred to me to write about the very thing Heidi and I used to play at when we were kids. The whole "getting lost and finding your way home" bid went over well with my agent friends out in New York and was quickly picked up. I'm on my second set of revisions for *The Redwood Forest,* and it looks like this will be the final round, thank God. No joke: Editing is a bore. The advance I got from my agency, however, makes it all worthwhile.

I thank Heidi on a daily basis for putting that bee in my bonnet a year ago.

I start the kettle for the hot water, leaning against the counter and pulling my sweater a little more tightly around my expanding belly, trying to ward off the chill. As if reminding me, the grandfather clock in the living room chimes four times, letting me know that Bryan will be home soon. He'll likely light a fire and then admonish me for helping carry in the firewood. He won't say it, but I think he's just as nervous as I am about the pregnancy going full-term, hence his apprehension on me lifting more than a spoon. My OB-GYN and I battle him weekly on the importance of exercise. This is a battle, I'm proud to say, we always win.

I prep my hot chocolate and flick on the radio. Janice Joplin's raspy voice cuts through the quiet of the house. Normally her voice would grate on my nerves, but "Down on Me" is a rare hit of hers that I'm actually down with.

I laugh at my own joke as I settle into a dining room chair, steaming mug warming my hands and music warming my heart.

The serenity of Humboldt was something I had to reinitiate myself into after eight years in New York. I thought I would miss it, the hustle and bustle of the Big Apple. But, strangely, I really don't. As it turns out, I'm much more partial to quiet than I had originally thought.

Any nostalgia I may have had over leaving New York has been tempered by the fact that I was able to keep my job writing for the pet product company. Thanks to the glories of the internet, I can still work for them remotely. It's a nice reprieve from working on my book. Mia was all too happy to hear about my move. Much like Heidi, she helped me pack up my belongings in New York like the loyal friend she is. We have a phone date every week and she's coming out next month to visit. It would appear I finally handled moving out correctly.

I sit and sip from my mug, letting my mind wander. Not a day goes by that I don't think about the message my mom left me, my father's indiscretions or the baby buried out on my property. I think it's the reason Bryan and I are so conscious about this pregnancy of mine: I want to do right by my dad's baby. And I want to do right by the baby I aborted.

Coming home certainly made me realize how much I had *not* come to terms with my abortion. I had thought I was happy in New York, "living the dream" as they say. I see now that I was barely living. Mia aside, I had no real friends. I worked day and night. And it was all over the guilt and self-loathing I had for myself over what happened junior year. I didn't know I could harbor such feelings for so long, but apparently I can.

But now, I see what happiness really is. It's living back at my old house with Bryan as my husband. It's seeing Heidi and Steph and Kyle almost every weekend.

It's spreading my creative wings and writing the story from my childhood playtime. It's the baby growing inside me.

I finish off my hot chocolate just as I spy Bryan's truck snaking up the long driveway. I watch him park and hop down from the cab, shrugging the hood of his jacket up over his head to protect him from the prevailing rain.

I vacate my chair and go to the front door just as Fats Domino starts crooning about hills filled with blueberries.

As I open it I can see, even through the raindrops that are coming down harder now, his eyes soften as he sees me standing at the threshold to our home with my hand protectively covering my belly. I can't help but smile.

"Happiness indeed," I whisper to the house.

It creeks, agreeing with me.

31932101R00090

Made in the USA
Lexington, KY
25 February 2019